"Have dinner with me tonight."

Instead of jumping at the invitation, Avery gave it some thought. The jungle drums would go into overdrive if she was seen socializing with the head of Mercom for the second time in one day.

"A plain, honest-to-God no will do," Jonas said dryly.

She shook her head. "I was about to say yes, but only if I cook something at home. I like to keep a low social profile."

"You're ashamed to be seen out with me," he accused.

She shot him a kindling look. "Do you want dinner at my place, or not?"

"You know damned well I do. Order in and I'll foot the bill."

"Good idea. You're not just a pretty face after all," she said in approval.

"That's you, Avery Crawford, not me...."

CATHERINE GEORGE was born in Wales, and early on developed a passion for reading, which eventually fueled her compulsion to write. Marriage to an engineer led to nine years in Brazil, but on his later travels the education of her son and daughter kept her in the U.K. And instead of constant reading to pass her lonely evenings, she began to write the first of her romance novels. When not writing and reading, she loves to cook, listen to opera, browse in antique shops and walk the Labrador.

THEIR SCANDALOUS AFFAIR

CATHERINE GEORGE

PREGNANCIES OF PASSION

HARLEQUIN®

TORONTO • NEW YORK • LONDON
AMSTERDAM • PARIS • SYDNEY • HAMBURG
STOCKHOLM • ATHENS • TOKYO • MILAN • MADRID
PRAGUE • WARSAW • BUDAPEST • AUCKLAND

ISBN-13: 978-0-373-82037-5
ISBN-10:   0-373-82037-2

THEIR SCANDALOUS AFFAIR

First North American Publication 2006.

Copyright © 2004 by Catherine George.

This edition published by arrangement with Harlequin Books S.A.

® and TM are trademarks of the publisher. Trademarks indicated with
® are registered in the United States Patent and Trademark Office, the
Canadian Trade Marks Office and in other countries.

www.eHarlequin.com

Printed in U.S.A.

CHAPTER ONE

THE early dinner had been a bad idea. The rest of the evening now yawned, with only the television in his hotel room for diversion. His own fault. One of his assistants should have made the trip. But occasionally the urge to escape from a desk was too powerful to resist. He smiled a little. Escape to a quiet market town was hardly a walk on the wild side.

He took out a pen and turned his newspaper over. He might as well stay in the bar until he'd finished the crossword. There was company of a sort here, at least.

But before he'd even solved the first clue everyone had left the bar at once in search of dinner. He shrugged. So much for company.

Four clues later he was juggling with an anagram when he noticed that company had arrived in the shape of a lone female. Tall and slender, but with curves in all the right places under a mannish suit, with dark hair pulled back from a narrow face. The matching dark eyes widened in dismay as she thrust a stray curl behind her ear with a hand that wore a diamond ring. Right hand, he noted in approval.

Unaware of the scrutiny, Avery Crawford made for the bar, her bright idea a lot less bright now she was actually here. With exasperating timing the room had emptied just before she arrived, leaving just one lone man reading a paper. Fat chance of fading into the background, then. She ordered mineral water from the barman, and sipped it as slowly as possible while she waited for people to arrive in search of pre-dinner drinks. This was one snag she hadn't expected. If no one turned up in time she would just have to sit at a table on her own. Unless…

She took a speculative look at the man engrossed in the evening paper. Rather nice. Six feet two, judging by the length of leg stretched out under the table, probably the usual eyes of blue, too, with that sun-streaked hair. A check with the time confirmed she was running out of it—fast— and, taking a chance that her quarry wasn't waiting for someone, she crossed the room to his table.

'Would you mind very much if I sat here?' she asked. 'I've bought my own drink, and I'm not trying to pick you up or sell you anything. I just need to be inconspicuous for a while. I counted on the place being crowded, so I could fade into the background, but my luck's out.'

'I'd be delighted,' he said promptly, indicating the chair beside him.

'Thank you.' She sat down, but shot up again at once in dismay. 'Your name's not Philip, by any chance?'

'Afraid not; it's Jonas. Jonas Mercer.' He half rose to give her a mock-formal bow.

'Thank heavens for that,' she said with relief, and sat down again. 'For one horrible moment I thought I'd blown it. How do you do? I'm Avery Crawford.'

His eyebrows rose above amused eyes as dark as her own. 'Why do you need company while you wait for the lucky Philip?'

'I'm not the one meeting him. I'm here as a sort of safety net for a friend.'

'Safety net?' he repeated, and sat back, relaxed, with the air of a man ready to be entertained. 'Go on.'

Avery hesitated. 'It's really my friend's story, not mine, but in the circumstances I don't suppose she'll mind. She's coming here soon to meet someone.'

'Then why does she need you along?'

'Frances is divorced, lonely sometimes, and in a wild moment put an ad in the local paper. ''Forty-something lady, slim, blonde, good sense of humour, would like to meet similar gentleman, etc.'' Philip is one of the men who answered. But once she'd actually arranged to meet him here she got cold feet, so I came up with a plan.'

He grinned. 'Let me guess! If she doesn't like him you rush to the rescue?'

'Exactly. Look,' she added, 'I must be keeping you from something. If you lend me your paper to hide behind I can leave you in peace.'

'I was just killing time before going up to my room here,' he assured her. 'Don't look now,' he added in an undertone. 'I think Philip may have arrived.'

The man eyeing the tables on his way to the bar had dark hair with a hint of silver at the temples, and wore a tweed jacket with a cut Avery's professional eye noted with respect.

'I hope you're right,' she muttered. 'He looks promising. The right age group, too. The others on the shortlist were a bit elderly. I warned Frances about that. A forty-something male is likely to go for a twenty-something female with a bra size bigger than her IQ. Three down is *chrysalis*, by the way.'

'So it is.' Jonas pencilled it in and glanced towards the door. 'Is this your friend?'

She glanced over her shoulder to see Frances White hesitating at the entrance, with the look of someone about to take to her heels and run. But the man waiting at the bar hurried forward, smiling. Avery buried her nose in the crossword again. 'I dare not look,' she whispered. 'What's happening?'

'They're sitting down together.'

'Does she seem happy?'

'They're both laughing.'

Avery chanced a quick look and smiled, relieved. 'My

back-up probably won't be needed. I should be able to go soon.'

'You can't leave yet!' said Jonas promptly. 'What's the drill if your friend wants out?'

'In a little while she'll make for the cloakroom, and I'll join her for instructions. When she goes back to Philip I ring her cellphone to announce some emergency, or, if Frances is happy to carry on, I just go home.'

Jonas Mercer shook his head. 'I've got a better idea. After you talk to your friend I buy you a real drink and we finish the crossword together while we keep tabs on the stay of play. Unless,' he added, 'there's someone waiting for you at home?'

'Not a soul.'

'Good.' His eyes held hers for an instant before they returned to the crossword. 'Just for the record, there's no one waiting for me, either. And sixteen down is *parapet*.'

She eyed his bent head in disbelief while he filled in the clue. No one waiting here in the hotel, maybe, but back home it was sure to be a different story.

'On your mark,' he murmured a couple of clues later. 'Your friend is on the move.'

Avery allowed time for Frances to reach their rendezvous, then got up too quickly and knocked her handbag over. Her companion jumped up to help her collect a few belongings, looming so much taller than expected as he straightened that Avery grinned, surprised.

'What's the joke?' he demanded.

'I'll tell you when I get back.' She strolled off, taking a quick look at Philip as she passed.

Frances was waiting impatiently for her. 'Who's the handsome stranger?'

'Never mind that—don't keep me in suspense. Is Philip interesting? Do you like him? Are you staying for a while or—?'

'All of the above. I'm having dinner with him.'

Avery whistled. 'Where?'

'Right here in the hotel. He booked a meal just in case.' Frances beamed as she patted Avery's hand. 'Thanks a lot, boss. Without you I'd have bottled out, which would have been a shame because Philip seems like a really charming man. And I think he likes me.'

'Of course he likes you, woman! Have fun and give me a full report tomorrow.'

'Are you going home now?'

Avery batted her eyelashes. 'I'm staying on for a drink with my handsome stranger first. So scoot. I'll see you in the morning.'

Avery renewed the discreet lipstick chosen for the operation, and thought about loosening her hair but with regret decided against it. Too obvious. She brushed a stray tendril back into the severe twist and rejoined Jonas.

He held out her cellphone. 'It escaped from your bag.'

'Thank you.' She looked round, but there was no sign of Frances and her date.

'They've gone,' he informed her.

'Philip's booked dinner here.'

'Then we can both relax. How about that drink?'

Avery asked for a glass of red wine, and eyed Jonas Mercer with frank curiosity as he went off to the bar to fetch it. Very tall and lean, with the muscular, co-ordinated look of someone who kept himself fit, he was attractive in a self-confident, all-male kind of way, rather than movie-star pretty. And in contrast to the decisive cut of his features there was a laid-back aura about him she found very appealing. Though normally she preferred her men dark and edgy. Men? She smiled bitterly. What men?

'Still smiling at your joke?' he asked, returning with her drink.

Avery looked blank for a moment, then laughed. 'Oh,

right. Earlier, when I was willing more people to arrive, I pegged you as "six feet two, eyes of blue", but I was wrong on both counts.'

'Only a couple of inches out. How about you? Five nine?'

'In my bare feet, yes. In heels I tower a bit.'

'Do you mind that?'

'Not any more.'

'But you did once?'

Avery raised an eyebrow as she sipped her drink. 'Twenty questions now, instead of crosswords?'

He slid the paper towards her. 'I finished it while you were away.'

'In that case there's no reason for me to stay.'

'There's a very compelling reason,' he said, and smiled at her. 'I'd like you to stay.'

'Then I will—for just a little while.' After literally forcing her company on him at the start Avery couldn't help feeling flattered that he wanted more of it. 'If I do will you ask more questions?'

He shrugged. 'It's what people do when they've just met. Indulge me. Tell me about Avery Crawford.'

She informed him that she was single, ran her own business, and owned a house on the outskirts of town. 'Your turn now.'

'Ditto, more or less,' said Jonas. 'I'm also single and own a house, but I help run the family business. I'm here on a reconnaissance trip. You live in a beautiful part of the world, Avery.'

She gave him a thumbnail sketch of the town, and told him to look out for the blue plaques which gave the past history of the older buildings, some of which dated back to the time of the Marcher lords. But as she finished her drink her stomach rumbled in ominous warning, reminding her she'd put no food in it since a sketchy breakfast.

With regret she got up before he could offer more wine,

which would not only go straight to her head but to other parts likely to cause embarrassment to both of them. 'Thank you for the drink, and for your invaluable help. Before I go, confess. What did you really think when I asked to join you?'

'That it was my lucky day,' he assured her promptly, and gave her a smile which took her breath away. 'Must you go? It's not late.'

'I really have to get home.'

'Then I'll see you to your car.'

When they reached it Avery held out her hand, smiling, and he clasped it firmly in his. 'Goodnight, Jonas. Thank you again.'

'It was my pleasure—' He broke off as someone called her name, and Avery waved to an acquaintance as she got in the car, raised a hand to Jonas Mercer and drove off.

She glanced in her mirror to see him standing on the hotel steps, and felt a lingering sensation she finally narrowed down to her body's reaction to the grasp of a hard male hand. No wonder it was unfamiliar. It was so long since she'd experienced anything like it that she drove home more slowly than usual, to savour the novelty.

Avery's pleasant glow vanished abruptly when her headlights picked out the man waiting in the porch at the front of her house.

'Hi,' said her visitor warily. 'Long time no see.'

She slammed the car door, eyeing him with hostility. 'What the devil are you doing here again, Paul?'

'Give me a break, Avery.' His handsome face lit with a persuasive smile. 'Let's be civilised and have a chat and a drink—or coffee, if you've had one too many at the Angel. Though, God knows, alcohol was never a weakness of yours.'

She stared at him with distaste as he slurred his words in a way she knew from past experience meant it was *he* who'd had one drink too many. 'How do you know I was at the Angel?'

'I saw you in the car park when I was leaving the pub across the road. I always sneak off there after a duty dinner with the parents. Who was the man?'

'What possible interest could that be to you?'

His face took on a hurt look. 'Do you have to be so damn belligerent, Avery? I'm here to do you a favour. Let me come in.'

'No way. Don't do this, Paul. I don't want you in my house—'

Before she could stop him he whipped the keys from her hand. He held her off as he unlocked the door, then cursed volubly as the burglar alarm sounded. 'Turn the bloody thing off, Avery!'

'No fear.' She smiled as sirens wailed in the distance. 'Better make yourself scarce, Paul, or I'll shop you to the police. Mummy and Daddy would just hate that.'

He hesitated, but as the sirens grew nearer he gave her a malevolent glare and made an unsteady run for the gate, tripping in his hurry to get away. Avery punched in the code for the alarm, smiling scornfully as the sirens receded into the distance. Paul Morrell had drunk too much to tell the difference between a police car and an ambulance making for the local hospital.

Her smile vanished as her cellphone rang. 'How did you get this number?' she snapped.

'By devious means,' said a deep, lazy voice very different from Paul Morrell's but instantly recognisable, even on short acquaintance.

'Oh.' Colour flew into her cheeks. 'I thought you were someone else.'

'This is Jonas Mercer. We met earlier,' he added helpfully.

'I know—I know. Sorry I snarled.'

'Something wrong?'

'Nothing at all. I'm fine. But how *did* you get my number?'

'When you left your phone behind I did some research.' There was a pause. 'Do you mind, Avery?'

'I suppose not,' she said slowly, rather surprised to find she didn't mind at all.

'Good. We were interrupted before I could ask to see you again. Have dinner with me tomorrow night.'

Avery stood very still, frowning at her reflection in the mirror. It was a long time since she'd accepted an invitation from a man, to dinner or anything else. She shrugged. Maybe it was time she did.

'I promise to save the crossword until we meet,' said Jonas.

'A generous offer!'

'Is that a yes?'

Suddenly the prospect of dinner with Jonas Mercer seemed like the perfect antidote to her encounter with Paul Morrell. 'Why not? Thank you. But not the Angel, please.'

'Your town; your choice. Just tell me when and where and I'll pick you up.'

But Avery wasn't about to give her address to a complete stranger, even one as appealing as Jonas Mercer. 'If you'll appear at the back door of the Angel about seven I'll chauffeur you to the Fleece. It's not far.'

'Thank you. I'll be waiting. Sleep well, Avery Crawford.'

She found she was smiling as she scrambled eggs later. And when she finally went yawning up to bed she felt pretty sure there would be no problem with insomnia after talking to Jonas Mercer—which was interesting. The encounter with a man she'd once been in love with had upset her so much she'd expected to lie awake all night, yet a few words from a virtual stranger and she was on an even keel again.

Avery slept so well she woke late the next morning and

rushed out without breakfast to drive into town. Her thriving business functioned in a small shop in a short row of others just like it in Stow Street, near the largest car park in town. Frances arrived just after her, in such a euphoric mood it was obvious the evening had gone well. But before Avery could demand every last detail the rest of her little team arrived and the phone started ringing. The working day was in full flow, and she was due at her first appointment of the day.

'I could be a while, Frances,' she said, on her way out. 'Squeezing Pansy Keith-Davidson into her grandmother's wedding gown will take some doing.'

'We'll all pray for generous seams!' Frances grinned conspiratorially. 'I'll fill you in about last night over lunch.'

Avery's appointment was with one of the wealthiest families in the neighbourhood. To her gratitude, she was pressed to coffee and pastries before embarking on an assignment so time-consuming it took up the entire morning.

'Quite a challenge,' she told Frances, when she finally joined her in the café in Stow Street for lunch. 'The bride's mother told me quite frankly that she'd had her heart set on yards of train and a designer label originally, but Pansy read some article in a bridal magazine and changed her mind at the last minute. Vintage numbers are the latest must have, and if the number once belonged to Grandma it wins the jackpot.'

'Can we do something with the dress?' said Frances.

'Oh, yes. It's a slinky satin number, in thirties Hollywood style, but darling Pansy's been on a punishing diet, so with inserts by you and some camouflaging embroidery from me all should be well. Mummy didn't turn a hair when I warned her about the cost involved.' Avery grinned. 'And Pansy was so thrilled with my ideas she begged me to make dresses for the six little bridesmaids she decided on only yesterday, would you believe? The snag is the time frame.

Due to the bride's U-turn we'll have to get our skates on. The wedding's next month.'

'We'll manage that, no problem. Nice morning's work, boss!'

'Now, then, enough shop talk.' Avery leaned forward, eyes sparkling. 'Tell me about last night.'

Frances smiled dreamily. 'It was lovely. Philip's such a charming man it's amazing he's been a widower so long. His married daughter made him answer the ad, and he's delighted now that she did.'

'So he should be. What does he do?'

'Accountant.'

'You liked him, obviously?'

'I took to him on sight—probably because he was almost as nervous as me to start with. But over dinner we talked non-stop, and he's asked me out again on Saturday.' Frances smiled radiantly. 'Thank you, Avery. I owe you.'

'Actually, you don't owe me a thing. I'm having dinner with Jonas Mercer, the man from the Angel bar, tonight.'

'*Really?*' Frances's eyes widened. 'My word, that's something new! What advantage does he have over the local male population?'

'The fact that he's not local, probably. But he's quite a charmer, too.' Avery grinned. 'I'll go halves for the ad you put in the paper.'

Avery rushed everyone off the premises dead on time that night, to get home to give her hair time to dry into its natural mane of exuberant curls. She fussed over her face more than usual, and changed her clothes twice before settling on jeans and a velvet jacket, irritated that she was behaving like an adolescent, and even more so when she found she'd arrived at the Angel car park a minute early.

But Jonas Mercer was there before her, in a khaki reefer

jacket and needlecord jeans which suited his lanky dimensions even better than the suit of the night before.

'Hello,' she said, smiling. 'You needn't have waited outside. You must be cold.'

'You said seven, and you strike me as a lady who means what she says.' He folded himself into the passenger seat and turned to her in awe. 'That's a glorious head of hair you've got there, Ms Crawford!'

Avery pulled a face. 'You wouldn't say that if you had to fight it tooth and nail to make it stay up every day.'

'Then why bother?'

'To present a businesslike image to my clients.'

He eased his legs out of her way as she changed gear. 'If your clients are men they'd prefer your hair the way it is now, believe me.'

'I deal mainly with women.' She described her morning in detail, amusing him with her tale of excited bride and stressed mother.

'I took a stroll round town this afternoon,' he told her, 'and I spotted Avery Alterations in the row of shops near the main car park.'

'That's headquarters, where the actual work goes on, but I travel to private homes to do the initial fittings. Here we are,' she added as the inn came into view.

She drove through an archway big enough to accommodate the coaches that had once rattled through it into the cobbled yard beyond. These days the Fleece's courtyard was full of cars, and Avery was pleased to find a space wide enough to park in easily. As they crossed the cobbles to the back entrance Jonas sniffed the air with anticipation.

'If the food matches the smells coming from the kitchen windows we're obviously in for a treat. Popular place,' he added as he followed Avery into the main bar. 'You bag the table by the window and I'll get the drinks. Red wine again?'

'Yes, please.'

The inn was buzzing, as usual, and Avery sat back, prepared to enjoy herself, confident that the meal, whatever they chose from the menu, would be good. She smiled in acknowledgement as someone waved to her, amused when more than one pair of curious eyes followed Jonas as he rejoined her. Avery Crawford, dining out with a man!

'This place has been serving food since the eighteenth century,' she told him. 'I had my first grown-up dinner here, as a treat for my eleventh birthday.'

'So you're a native of these parts? How long has Avery Alterations been functioning?'

'In one form or another for about twenty-five years.'

Jonas eyed her in surprise. 'The sums don't add up.'

'My mother started it up at home when I was small. She was a qualified tailor and taught me everything I know. Eventually I was able to make my own dresses for my university balls.'

'Clever lady.' Jonas leaned nearer as the noise level increased. 'Was your degree in fine art?'

'No, maths.'

He grinned. 'Snap—mine too. Right, then, Ms Crawford, you're the expert here. What do you recommend?'

Once they'd given their orders Avery eyed her companion expectantly. 'So what did you do after you graduated?'

Jonas Mercer sat back, relaxed. 'After a gap-year backpacking round the world, supposedly studying other people's transport systems, I joined the family business, as I'd always intended. Once he was sure I was up to scratch, my father decided on semi-retirement. With his guiding hand, I help run the show pretty much as it's been run for decades—independent of help from bank or City. We're in haulage, warehousing, some construction work, and so on. Remunerative, but not exciting,' he added.

'I think any successful business run for that length of time with no outside financial help is very exciting indeed,' Avery assured him. 'I used to work in the City, once upon a time.'

His eyebrows rose. 'Did you, indeed? Why did you leave?'

'I'll tell you some other time—our dinner's approaching.'

Over the meal, which was as excellent as Avery had promised, Jonas made no effort to press her about her change of career. Instead he talked about his mother's passion for gardening and his father's golf handicap, and the various Mercer relatives who worked with him.

'I have plenty of help to carry the load,' he said wryly. 'Would you like coffee?'

Coffee had an air of finality about it. And because this type of evening was missing from her life these days Avery was reluctant to let it end yet. She hesitated for a moment, then suggested they go back to her place for the coffee.

'If you're willing to walk back into town afterwards,' she added. 'It's not far.'

'I'd like that very much,' he said promptly, and signalled to a waiter for the bill.

When they arrived at the four-square Victorian villa of Avery's birth, Jonas looked on in approval as she switched off the alarm. 'A sensible precaution if you live alone. Do you?' he added casually, looming tall in the narrow hallway.

'Yes.' She raised an eyebrow. 'Or did you think I was after some light entertainment while the man in my life is away?'

He shook his head, unperturbed. 'I was thinking more of relatives.'

Her eyes shadowed as she led the way down the long narrow hall to the kitchen at the back of the house. 'Not any more.'

'It's a lot of house for one,' Jonas commented as he followed her into the large, welcoming room.

She nodded. 'I had thoughts about selling or letting it when it came to me. But it's been in the family since my great-grandparents took possession of it from new, and in the end I decided to stay put because at first I ran the business from home.' Avery switched on the kettle, and shot a look at the man lounging at ease in one of the rush-seated chairs, his endless legs stretched out under the table. 'Would you prefer something else to coffee? Whisky, brandy—?'

He smiled. 'Would it destroy my image forever to ask for a cup of tea?'

Which, Avery assumed, was his way of saying he had no misconceptions about what else was on offer. 'Tea it is—in which case we ought to drink it out of my mother's best china cups in the sitting room.'

'I'd rather stay here. So what did you actually do in the City?' he added as he watched her pour boiling water onto tea bags.

'I was regarded as something of a prodigy. By the age of twenty-five I was a fund manager for one of the big insurance groups, handling billions in retail and pension-funds assets.'

'High-flyer,' said Jonas with respect.

'So was Icarus! But instead of flying too near the sun, like him, I left the City because my mother was ill.' Avery's face was sober as she set two steaming mugs on the table. 'So what exactly brings you to this neck of the woods, Mr Mercer?' she asked, taking the chair opposite.

'My father heard of some reasonable land in this area. I'm here to check it out for building purposes.'

Avery welcomed the idea if it meant return visits by Jonas Mercer. 'And is the site suitable?'

'I've come up against one or two snags, but I'll iron them out before I leave.' Something in the dark eyes belied the indolence of his posture. 'I'd like to see you again before I do.'

'When do you go?'

'Friday, if all goes to plan.'

She thought about it for a moment. 'I'm free on Thursday.'

'I suppose it's too much to hope for tomorrow evening as well?'

She shook her head regretfully. 'I'm committed to a day of eye-crossing hand work tomorrow. I'll be slaving away on it at home all day, and by evening I'll be grumpy and tired, and no fit company for anyone.'

'In that case—' Jonas drained his mug and got up '—I'd better let you get to bed to shape up for it, and I'll take myself off to practice patience until Thursday.'

'I'll look forward to that. Thank you for dinner, Jonas. I enjoyed the evening very much.' To her surprise Avery felt flustered as she led the way to the front door. She was no schoolgirl on a first date, she reminded herself irritably. Of course he wasn't going to kiss her goodnight.

But Jonas took her by the shoulders and bent his head to prove her wrong, with a kiss which packed such a punch her knees were trembling when he released her. He looked down at her for a long moment, and then kissed her again very thoroughly. At last he raised his head, trailed a finger down her flushed cheek, and smiled down into her startled eyes.

'I'll be here at seven on the dot. Goodnight, Avery Crawford.'

CHAPTER TWO

WHEN Avery made the decision to keep on her mother's business she'd advertised for an experienced tailor and Frances White had entered her life—first as an employee, but soon as a valued friend. With Frances's input the business had rapidly expanded enough to need premises in town, at which point Avery had engaged two former schoolfriends as skilled part-time help. This new arrangement had left Avery free to concentrate on the financial and advertising side, and on visits to clients for fittings. She had also been able to fine-tune her own particular talent for the embroidery and delicate hand repairs Avery Alterations had soon become known for in the neighbourhood. And if she sometimes yearned for the buzz and adrenaline of her past life in the City, Avery kept it strictly to herself.

She was in mellow mood next day as she settled down in the small spare room to work on Pansy Keith-Davidson's vintage bridal gown. Unpicking seams in delicate fabric was tedious, time-consuming work, and normally Avery worked with the radio for company, or an audio book—preferably a thriller. But today she was thinking exclusively of Jonas Mercer—and his kisses. In the past she'd had her fair share of them, just like any other half-presentable female, but lately they hadn't featured in her life at all. She knew there was more to it than that. With just a kiss or two Jonas Mercer had revived feelings she'd been utterly certain she would never experience again.

Avery found her hands had stilled, and she was staring blindly at ivory slipper satin instead of treating it with the respect it deserved. She pulled herself together sharply, switched on her thriller and focused her full attention on the work which represented a handsome fee for Avery Alterations.

It was late, and Avery's eyes felt hot and dry by the time careful ironing had completed her day's work. As she stepped out of the shower her phone rang, and she snatched it off the bathroom stool.

'Good evening, Ms Crawford. Are you cross-eyed and grumpy?' enquired a familiar voice.

'I was by the time I finished for the day, Mr Mercer, but I'm better now,' she informed him, rubbing at her hair.

'Good. Have you spotted the coincidence in today's crossword? Four across—"The architect of King Minos's labyrinth at Crete."'

'Daedalus, who just happened to be Icarus's daddy,' she said smugly. 'But some people work too hard to dally with crosswords, Mr Mercer.'

'I stand reproved! I booked a table at the Walnut Tree, by the way, subject to your approval.'

'I'm impressed. I've never been, but I'm more than happy to try it,' she assured him.

'It's a fair distance away, so it means an early start. I'll call for you at seven,' he said again.

'I'll make a point of getting home on time.'

'Here's my cell number if you need to contact me.'

'Hang on, I'll get a pen.' Avery ran into the bedroom and scribbled on the telephone pad on her bedside table. 'Got it.'

'Good. Thank you for taking pity on a lonely stranger last night, Avery.'

'I enjoyed the evening very much,' she assured him.

'So did I. Very much indeed. We'll do it all again tomorrow. Goodnight, Avery.'

She felt very pleased with life after Jonas's phone call, even after a look through her wardrobe—which confirmed that she owned far more in the way of business suits and jeans than anything frivolous. With no time to run something up, the only option was the dateless little black dress most women owned as standby. Jonas wouldn't know—or care—that it dated from her City days.

Frances rang later, to report on the day. 'Quite a bit of new work came in, but it's just routine stuff. We can fit it in around the wedding order.'

'Thanks, Frances. I've finished the first phase on the gown. Over to you tomorrow.'

'Brilliant—but no resting on your laurels, boss. Mrs K-D rang this afternoon, asking if you could spare the time to have tea with her tomorrow afternoon to measure the bridesmaids. I said you'd ring to confirm.'

Avery groaned. 'Lucky me! I'll ring her now.'

Later, supper eaten and chores done, Avery wished that she'd said yes to this evening with Jonas Mercer after all. She liked him enormously for someone she'd known only a day or so.

After leaving university, where she'd played as hard as anyone else and worked a lot harder than most, her career in a male-dominated world in the City had inevitably brought her into contact with a lot of men. She'd disliked some intensely, liked others in a temperate kind of way, and during her time in London had been involved in two relationships that had been anything but temperate. But this instant rapport with Jonas was—different.

She heaved a sigh as she switched on her computer. Doing accounts was a poor substitute for an evening spent with the deeply appealing Mr Mercer.

When Avery arrived at the shop next morning she handed the garment box to Frances, went through the pile of mail, and found a letter that sent her high spirits into a nosedive. Morrell Properties were not renewing her lease. The premises must be vacated by the end of the next calendar month.

'What's up?' said Frances, eyeing her face.

Avery showed her the letter. 'My landlords are evicting

me. They've never given me more than a half-yearly lease at a time, so I suppose this was always on the cards.'

And now she knew the reason for Paul Morrell's visit. His father owned Morrell Properties, and Paul had persuaded him to lease the Stow Street premises to her in the first place. At the time Avery hadn't cared much for the six-monthly terms, and even less for feeling beholden to Paul Morrell. But nothing else had been available in town at the time, and no businesswoman worth her salt could have passed up premises at an affordable rent in a good commercial location.

'So what happens now?' asked Frances.

'We have a month and a bit to find new premises, and if the worst comes to the worst we'll work from my place after that until I find something else in town,' said Avery, sounding more positive than she felt. 'Break the news when Louise and Helen arrive, but tell them there's nothing to worry about.'

She shut herself into the minuscule cloakroom, rang a number in the City of London, and for the first time in three years asked for Paul Morrell's extension.

'Morrell,' he said crisply, sounding very different from the man she'd seen off two evenings before.

'Avery Crawford,' she stated, equally crisp.

'*Avery?*' he said incredulously. 'God, how wonderful to hear from you. This is the most extraordinary coincidence. I was about to ring you to apologise for coming to your place in that state—'

'You shouldn't have been there in any state, but never mind the apologies. This isn't a social call. I take it you came to tell me your father is evicting me?'

'If you must put it like that, yes—though it isn't really eviction, Avery. The terms of your lease were clear from the start. I spotted you in town and decided to break the news before you got it in the post. I scorched rubber through the back streets to Gresham Road, because I knew you wouldn't even open the door to me if you got home first.'

'A strong possibility,' she agreed dryly. 'But if you drove that fast you're lucky you weren't picked up by the police.'

'Tell me about it! I cruised to my parents' house so slowly afterwards it was a wonder I wasn't nicked for kerb crawling.' He paused. 'I tried to persuade my father to give you more notice, Avery, but he's selling the land—which includes the shops.'

Avery waited a moment, then asked the question which was her sole reason for contacting Paul Morrell again in this life. 'Who's buying?'

'The Mercom Group. I asked around, but no one knows much about them in the City. Pretty solid outfit, though. They've been in business since before the war. Haulage, warehousing and so on—are you still there, Avery?'

'Yes, I'm still here.' She heard voices in the background, then Paul spoke again.

'Avery, I've got to go. I'm due at a meeting.' His voice lowered urgently. 'I'm really glad you rang, darling. Does this mean—?'

'Absolutely not,' she said flatly. 'All I wanted was information.'

There was a pause, then she heard Paul heave a sigh. 'I wish to God I could put the clock back. I was a fool,' he said bitterly.

'No, Paul. I was the fool.'

Avery disconnected and sat staring into space, cursing herself for getting a man wrong yet again. Jonas Mercer was the first man in years to appeal to her on a man/woman level. Unfortunately he also happened to run the company that would probably demolish the row of shops that included Avery Alterations—which it had every right to do. But that wasn't the point. The part that infuriated her—and cut surprisingly deep—was the discovery that Jonas had known all

along how the deal would affect her business but hadn't
seen fit to tell her.

When Avery went back into the shop Louise came running in from the café next door. 'Hey, what do you think?'
she said breathlessly. 'None of the other shops got a letter
about the lease.'

'Really?' Avery's eyes narrowed ominously. 'How very
interesting.'

Frances exchanged a speaking look with the other two,
and briskly requested Avery's help in fitting the inserts
she'd cut to stitch into the vintage bridal gown. There was
a steady influx of customers from then on, and for the rest
of the day Avery was kept so busy that Frances advised her
to go straight home after her session with the bridesmaids.

'No point in trekking back here afterwards. I'll lock up.'

Avery thanked her and smiled encouragingly at her little
team as she left. 'Don't worry. I'll soon find other premises
to rent.'

Avery's session with six excited little girls and their
harassed mothers took up so much time and energy that it
was late by the time she left. Several times during the day
she'd been on the point of ringing Jonas, but in the end
decided to allow herself the satisfaction of confronting him
in person. She arrived home to find Jonas there before her,
standing tall in the arched porch like a sentry in a box.

'Hello, Avery, you're late,' he said, moving swiftly to
open the car door. 'The table's booked for eight.'

She got out, ignoring his helping hand. 'Cancel it,' she
said tersely. 'I'm not hungry.'

He stepped back, frowning. 'What's wrong?'

'I'll tell you inside.' She unlocked the door and punched
in the code for the alarm. 'In here, please.'

She ushered him into a dauntingly formal room, with pic-
tures and furnishings dating from her grandparents' day. The
only modern features were two central heating radiators so

rarely switched on that the temperature of the room was as arctic as Avery's manner.

'Do sit down,' she said politely, but Jonas shook his head and drew himself to his full, formidable height, moving to one side to avoid the coloured glass chandelier Avery's grandparents had brought back from a holiday in Venice.

'I'll stand.'

'Then I'll come straight to the point.' Avery looked up at him coldly. 'I gather that this "family firm" of yours has purchased the land which includes the shops on Stow Street.'

His mouth tightened. 'So that's it. Who the hell leaked that? It hasn't been made public yet.'

'I received a letter from Morrell Properties today, telling me my lease won't be renewed, so I made a few enquiries.' Her eyes speared his. 'You've known about this all along. Why didn't you tell me?'

'I fully intended to the minute planning permission was confirmed,' he said curtly. 'It didn't come through officially until late this afternoon.'

'Oh.' Avery felt herself deflate like a pricked balloon. 'I see.'

His eyes hardened. 'I must have a word with George Morrell. I told him I wanted to inform all the leaseholders in person before they received an official letter.'

She smiled faintly. 'None of the other leaseholders received a letter today. Only me.'

Jonas frowned. 'You're saying this is personal?'

'You bet it is.'

'Why?'

'His son arranged the lease for me in the first place as a favour, even though Daddy disapproved.' Avery's chin lifted. 'I'm considered ineligible as a friend for the Morrell son and heir. In fact, I've been expecting this kind of letter every time the lease comes up for renewal, so that part of it was no shock.' She looked at him squarely. 'But because

I liked you I was angry—hurt, even—to find you'd kept me in the dark about the deal.'

'Avery—' His phone rang, and with a muttered curse Jonas answered it, his face grim as he rapped out questions to his caller. He snapped the phone shut, looking bleak. 'Sorry, I have to go. There's been an accident involving one of our vehicles.'

'Was anyone hurt?'

'Yes. I'll drive straight to the hospital.' He took an envelope from his pocket as they reached the outer door. 'I intended to give you this as a parting gift at the end of a very different evening. Read it when I'm gone.' He hesitated, and for a moment she thought—and hoped—that he would kiss her. But he merely looked at her for a moment, then turned away without touching her. 'Goodbye, Avery.'

After her usual locking and bolting routine Avery stared in blank dismay as she read the letter which had been faxed through to Jonas after planning had been confirmed. Mercom, it seemed, had no intention of demolishing the shops in Stow Street. The leaseholders were being offered the option either to purchase, or to lease their premises from their new landlord. There were plans to build on the land behind them, but construction work would not affect trading. Traffic access to the building site would be via Cheap Street, to the north of the car park. Official confirmation would be forwarded to Miss Crawford in due course.

Avery stalked round the kitchen like an angry tigress, heaping curses on George Morrell's head. His indecent hurry to terminate her lease had put paid to what might have developed into a beautiful friendship with Jonas Mercer. She gave a short, mirthless laugh. Who was she kidding? For the first time in years she would have liked more than that. But fat chance of friendship or anything else now Jonas had gone speeding back home to—to where, exactly? She looked at the letter-heading. Mercom was based in Kew, in London, but she had no idea of Jonas's private address. A call to his cellphone was the only way to contact him, but she couldn't see herself doing that any time soon.

'No problem, everyone,' Avery announced next morning. 'I merely pay rent to a new landlord.' She reported on her meeting with a Mercom representative, and it was only later, over lunch with Frances, that she revealed the identity of their new landlord.

'I went straight for the jugular because he kept me in the dark about it,' she said disconsolately, 'and then he handed me this.' She passed the Mercom letter to Frances, who smiled in relief as she finished reading it.

'So we're not out in the snow after all, boss dear! I trust you grovelled suitably to Mr Mercer afterwards?'

'I didn't get the chance. He had to rush off to cope with an emergency back at base.' Avery heaved a sigh. 'I doubt I'll see him again.'

Embroidery was a pastime she normally found therapeutic, but that day it gave Avery far too much scope for brooding over Jonas. And to her frustration she soon realised that her work was unnecessary. Frances was so skilled a tailor that the inserts had no need of disguise, and after the first couple of hours Avery wished she'd kept her big mouth shut and never mentioned embroidery to the bride. A whole morning of working ivory silk flowers and leaves on ivory satin was as much as she could take, and at lunchtime Avery gave herself a break.

To Avery's infinite gratitude she found that Louise and Helen had worked like beavers to finish an order for miles of curtain for a client's barn conversion, and had already started cutting the shell-pink taffeta delivered that morning for the bridesmaids' dresses. Frances was completing skilled alterations to a man's suit, and Avery, glad of company while she worked, began on the repair of a black lace evening dress promised for the weekend.

Any hope of hearing personally from Jonas gradually

faded as ten days passed, with only official communications from solicitors to Avery about the leasing of the Stow Road premises from Mercom. By the following weekend work was completed on the wedding set, including a last-minute alteration to the couture coat and dress bought by the bride's mother, who had dropped a dress size since the purchase.

Avery received a very generous cheque when she made her delivery to the delighted recipients, accepted tea in preference to the offered champagne, then drove back to town to bank the cheque before transferring all outstanding work from the shop to Gresham Street for the weekend, as usual.

On Saturday evening Avery walked into town to join the others in the park for the usual Bonfire Night display of fireworks put on for charity, and later, after Louise and Helen had waved their husbands and children off, the four women made for a new wine bar the other side of town to enjoy a meal. Avery was buying, as thanks for the extra work put in to get the wedding order finished on time.

'I'm surprised you had a Saturday evening free, Frances,' teased Avery over the meal.

'I told Philip he'd have to wait until tomorrow,' said her friend, and smiled smugly. 'He's cooking Sunday lunch for me at his place.'

'You mean the man cooks, as well?' said Helen enviously. 'Can I send my Tom round to him for lessons?'

Avery joined in the laughter, pleased that life had taken an upward turn for her friend, but on the leisurely stroll home she couldn't help feeling wistful as she thought of Frances spending Sunday with her Philip. Avery Crawford would spend hers as usual—catching up on laundry and household chores.

As she watched a late burst of fireworks light the sky nearby she thought with nostalgia of Sundays past, some spent at home with her mother for a rest and some home cooking, others in London, where she'd been part of a group of friends who ate brunch together, or drove into the country to some eating place reviewed in the Sunday glossies. But when she'd met Paul he'd demanded her undivided attention. By the time their relationship had ended Avery's group of friends had dispersed to different jobs and locations, and she'd been needed at home with her mother.

There'd been no time for socialising during that first harrowing year. It had taken all Avery's time and energy to keep the business going while she cared for her mother, who'd insisted on keeping to the work she loved as long as she could, despite a rapidly deteriorating heart condition. Before the year was out Ellen Crawford had been dead, and, swamped and sodden with grief, Avery's first instinct had been to run away, back to her life in the City. But out of loyalty to her mother she'd stayed on to complete standing orders, and coped with more work as it came in. Eventually she had decided that as a fitting memorial to her mother she would expand the business. And now, two years on, it was a commercial success. But Avery was increasingly conscious of a lack in her life.

She sighed. This was Jonas Mercer's fault. He was the catalyst. She had long ago given up any idea of returning to the City. That part of her life was over. And until she'd forced her company on Jonas at the Angel she'd been content to jog along in the comfortable little rut she'd made for herself back in her home town. He was the first man in years to raise even a spark of interest in her. Not that there was any hope of seeing him again. The heir apparent of Mercom would send underlings to the town in future.

Avery came out of her reverie to realise that the smell of smoke was growing stronger. And the glow in the sky was too constant for fireworks. With sudden dread she began to run. As she skirted the deserted cattle market a group of youths rushed past her in the opposite direction. One of them tripped, his anguished face clearly visible for a moment under the street lamp before he fled after the others. A blood-curdling wail of sirens filled the air, and Avery raced in panic towards the glow—then gave a screech of horror as the Stow Street shops came into view. The betting shop next to Avery Alterations was on fire.

By the time she'd been allowed through the cordon at the actual scene the Fire Brigade and the police were in full control, and Sergeant Griffiths turned from consultation with one of his constables to make sure Avery kept well back as hoses were directed at the betting shop.

'Don't worry, Avery, the fire's already contained,' he said firmly. 'The betting shop's in pretty bad shape, but yours is intact, as far as I can tell. You'll have smoke damage, though.'

'Any idea what happened?' she panted, gasping for breath.

'PC Sharp's just been talking to the manager of the Red Lyon on Cheap Street. Apparently some lads were letting off fireworks on the waste ground behind the shops earlier. One of their rockets must have gone through the betting shop roof.' He smiled grimly. 'One of them had a social conscience and rang for the Fire Brigade before they scarpered.'

Avery turned to smile in rueful sympathy as Harry Daniels, the betting shop manager, came running to join them. 'How are you, Harry?' she asked, as he stared, stunned, at his blackened premises.

He turned to her, shaking his head. 'Bloody furious, love. I'd like to get my hands on the little devils that did this!'

'Now, then, no vigilante stuff, Harry,' warned Sergeant Griffiths. 'Leave it to the professionals.'

Eventually the fire chief told Avery she could make an inspection, and, escorted by two firefighters armed with torches, Avery looked round her premises, her heart sinking as she examined the smoke damage on the wall shared with the betting shop.

'Don't worry—no broken glass or structural damage,'

said one of her hefty young escorts. 'Just needs a lick of paint on the party wall.'

'Better check on the sewing machines,' warned his colleague.

Avery thanked them warmly. 'I'll take them home with me. And as much fabric as possible.'

There were plenty of willing hands to stow the bolts of cloth and two of the machines in her car, and to save a return trip for Avery the sergeant ordered one of his constables to transport the other machines, and anything else she wanted, to Gresham Road.

It was nearly four in the morning before Avery said goodbye to the constable, who had insisted on making tea for her before doing his fetching and carrying. Avery thanked him warmly as he left and finally trudged off to bed, heaping curses on Guy Fawkes for leaving a legacy of firework displays and bonfires every November 5th from 1605 onwards.

After what felt like only a few minutes' sleep the phone woke her up again.

Oh, God—what now? 'Hello?' she croaked.

'Avery?' said an urgent voice.

'Yes?'

'Jonas Mercer. Are you all right?'

'Oh, hi. Yes, yes—I'm fine.' She cleared her throat and struggled upright. 'Unlike my shop.'

'Never mind the blasted shop,' he said roughly. 'Were you there when the fire started?'

'Not in the shop. I was walking home from the other side of town. I saw the blaze in the distance and ran like the wind when I heard sirens. It was a lot worse for the betting shop. Harry Daniels, the manager, was still in shock when I left for home with my sewing machines—well, with two of them. Tony brought the rest.'

'Who's Tony?'

'A strapping young police constable who heaved all my

other machines into the house and even made me a cup of tea.'

'Good for him.' There was silence for a moment. 'I'll be there to make an inspection tomorrow. I assume you carry insurance?'

'Of course.'

'Good. I need to do some juggling with my diary first thing tomorrow. I'll ring you some time during the morning to fix a time.'

'Jonas—'

'Yes?'

'Thank you.'

Avery rang off without specifying what she was thanking him for, and heaved herself out of bed to make for the bathroom, where the red-eyed, pallid apparition in the mirror sent her diving into the shower.

While she sluiced the smell of smoke from her hair Avery made a mental list of things to do. Normally Frances would have been the first one to contact, but knowing that her friend would rush round right away, instead of going off to lunch with Philip, Avery rang Helen instead. And, just as she'd hoped, Helen's husband—who serviced their machines on a regular basis—was good-natured enough to give up part of his Sunday to lend a helping hand.

Avery left a message on Louise's phone, then threw on jeans and a sweater and managed to swallow some coffee before Tom Bennett arrived with his anxious young wife in tow.

'We packed the boys off to Tom's parents for Sunday lunch, so I came to help,' announced Helen. 'Gosh, Avery, what a shock! Are you OK?'

'I'm fine. But poor Harry Daniels was in quite a state last night.'

'Do they know who did it?'

'Some local lads let off fireworks on the waste ground

behind Stow Street. A rocket must have got out of hand and set fire to the betting shop roof.'

'And they ran off without being identified, of course,' said Tom, and hoisted his tool bag. 'Right then, Avery. Bring on the machines.'

She led him to the dining room, now transformed into a temporary workshop. 'I'd brought the outstanding orders home for the weekend as usual, thank God, and the wedding gear had already been delivered to the Keith-Davidsons.'

Helen shuddered. 'Just imagine those frilly pink taffeta jobs covered in black soot.'

'Don't! By the way, I brought all the bolts of fabric home I could. Let's have a look at them.'

After every yard of it had been examined Avery decided that after a few lengths had been cut off each roll the rest of the fabric would be fit to use again in an emergency.

'But the insurance will cover replacements, so I'll order more right away.'

The machines were eventually confirmed as in good working order, and after making a big fry-up for a late lunch Avery saw her helpers off, resolving to buy Tom a bottle of the most expensive single malt she could find by way of thanks.

She was yawning over her insurance policy later when Louise rang.

'What's up, Avery? We've just got back from Sunday lunch with the parents.'

When Avery had explained Louise exclaimed in horror, and promised to be at the house first thing in the morning. 'Does Frances know?'

'No. I couldn't spoil her lunch with Philip. I'll ring her this evening.'

'It might be a good idea to do it sooner than that. She might hear it from someone else before then.'

Louise was right. Frances heard it on the local radio while she was helping Philip clear up, and rang before Avery could contact her, fizzing with indignation that she hadn't been informed sooner.

'Why spoil your day, Frances? There's nothing for you to do at this point. Tom came round to check the machines, and Helen came with him to help—'

'Louise, too, I suppose?' said Frances ominously.

'No, she was with her family at Sunday lunch with Grandma as usual. I've only just spoken to her. Don't be cross. Please.' To her embarrassment Avery's voice cracked, and Frances, immediately contrite, assured her she was worried, not cross.

'I'll be there in five minutes—'

'You most certainly will not! Enjoy the rest of your day with Philip. I had no sleep to speak of last night, and I'm desperate for a good long nap.'

'If you're sure?' said Frances doubtfully.

'Very sure. I appreciate the offer, but I'll need you far more in the morning.'

Avery had been telling the simple truth about needing a nap. She stacked the dishwasher, made herself some tea, and sat at the table with the Sunday paper to drink it. When she found her eyes were crossing she trudged up to her room, then groaned in frustration. Her bed reeked of smoke.

After she'd heaved the mattress over and put fresh linen on it she was reeling with fatigue. She undressed, and crawled under her duvet at last, feeling as though she could sleep until next morning. And when she woke at long last, she found to her astonishment that she had.

CHAPTER THREE

AFTER the longest sleep she'd had in years Avery felt a lot better by the time her workforce arrived, raring to go with whatever was demanded of them. Helen and Louise started work at once on the most urgent jobs, with the stock of thread kept in the house, while Avery drove to town with Frances to see what could be salvaged from the shop.

Frances exclaimed in horror when they arrived in Stow Street. The betting shop stood out like a blackened stump in a row of perfect teeth. The other shopkeepers, out in force to view the damage, greeted Avery with sympathy. But to her relief she found that by daylight the damage to her own premises was less extensive than expected.

'It looked so awful by torchlight I was ready to abandon the place and find somewhere else,' Avery said, as she investigated. 'I'm not sure about the electricity yet, so we'd better not try it.'

'It's just the one wall that looks so bad, but with a thorough cleaning and some fresh paint the place can soon be sorted,' said Frances firmly, and went into the storeroom to check on supplies of cotton and thread. She emerged triumphant. 'It's all fine.'

Avery breathed a sigh of relief. 'Let's get as much as possible back to the ranch, then.' She stuck a typed notice in a prominent place in the window—to inform her usual customers, and any new ones, that business would carry on as usual at 14 Gresham Road until repairs were made in Stow Street—and went outside to study the effect.

'Don't worry,' said Frances. 'The others will keep a lookout for stray customers. We shouldn't lose too much business.'

'I hope you're right,' said Avery. 'A Mercom representative is arriving some time today in person to sort things out.'

Frances shot her a glance as she got in the car. 'Is that who I think it is?'

Avery nodded. 'Jonas Mercer in person.'

'Well, well—so it's not all bad news, then! Make sure you grovel.'

It was a hectic morning. After Avery's consultation with her insurance company constant phone calls came in, with messages of sympathy from friends and regular customers. Expecting every call to be from Jonas, she grew edgier by the minute as the morning wore on—a fact commented on when the owner of the smartest dress shop in town arrived to commiserate.

'You look a bit stressed, darling,' said Christine Porter. 'I volunteered to bring the weekly delivery so I could check on you. Here you are, girls.' She handed over two garment bags of clothes. 'We did good trade on Saturday. I've promised most of the shortening jobs by Friday, as usual. But there's a jacket to alter for you, Frances, and an evening gown and a very pricey knitted coat in need of your particular magic touch, Avery. No sweat; the customer is willing to wait. Charge what you like.'

Avery sighed. 'I may have to if it takes time. Want some coffee?'

Christine declined regretfully. 'Must go back now I know you're all fine. I'm glad there wasn't too much damage to your shop,' she added, and gave a little shiver. 'Thank heavens the little devils didn't fire a rocket through my place.'

Avery took the garments up to the dress rail she kept in

her sewing room, and groaned as she hung up a bead-encrusted evening gown with layers of chiffon skirt and a white knitted coat—both of which would take hours of work to shorten by hand. She went to her bedroom to renew the lipstick she'd chewed off during the morning, and spun round in alarm when Frances burst into her room without knocking.

'Come down quickly. He's here!' she hissed, pulling Avery from the room.

'Who's here?'

'Mr Mercer, the representative from Mercom, has just arrived,' said Frances, in tones meant to carry to the man standing in the hall below. She gave Avery a dig in the ribs and whispered, *'Grovel!'*

Avery strolled downstairs, smiling brightly as Jonas moved forward to meet her, immaculate and imposing in a suit which fitted so perfectly it was obviously custom-made. 'Good morning.'

'Good morning, Miss Crawford,' he said briskly. 'I hoped you could spare an hour for a working lunch.'

'Now?'

His lips twitched as the long-case clock beside him chimed the half-hour after noon. 'As good a time as any.'

'Of course,' she said politely. 'Will you hold the fort, Frances?'

'With pleasure,' said her friend promptly.

Avery walked out of the house telling herself that she was twenty-eight—well, twenty-nine—years old, and it was utterly stupid to behave like such a *girl* because Jonas Mercer had turned up out of the blue to surprise her instead of ringing to make an appointment. She wasn't a dentist.

'How are you, Avery?' he asked, as he handed her into a sleek, dangerous-looking piece of machinery very different from the modest estate car she'd bought to accommodate dress rails full of garments.

'I'm fine now. It's surprising what a good night's sleep will do. I had very little on Saturday night.'

'I can well believe it.'

'I'm glad of this opportunity to thank you,' she told Jonas later, as they turned into the cobbled courtyard of the Fleece. 'Your plans for Stow Street, I mean. I apologise for jumping to the wrong conclusion last time we met.'

'You were one angry lady,' he said wryly, and casually reversed the car into a space Avery would never have attempted. 'I've booked a room here this time.'

So he was here for one night, at least. 'I've heard that it's very comfortable.'

'It's bound to have one disadvantage,' he said blandly. 'I doubt that a beautiful woman will ask to share my table tonight.'

Not this one, anyway, thought Avery with regret. 'You never know your luck.'

Jonas reached into the back of the car for a newspaper, and brandished it at her as they crossed the cobbles. 'I left the crossword for you. Or have you solved it already?'

Avery eyed him with scorn. 'With the kind of day I'm having?'

He glanced down at her. 'You're wound up pretty tight, Ms Crawford.'

'With good reason,' she reminded him as they reached the bar.

'Red wine?' asked Jonas.

'Not during a working day. Mineral water and a ham sandwich, please. I'd better grab that table over there. I can't stay too long.'

From her seat by the window Avery watched him chatting to the barman, amused when she realised that her grey pin-striped trouser suit was almost the twin of the one worn by Jonas. For once fate had been kind enough to let her look well groomed before he arrived, if not in the best of tempers. Waiting for his phone call had put her in a bad mood.

Frances's order to grovel had been timely. Avery gave a mental shrug. Her apology had not been exactly impassioned, but she'd made it. And now, with time to view Jonas Mercer objectively, she felt the same irresistible tug of attraction. His tan had faded, and his hair was darkening to what was probably its winter shade of tawny brown. It was thick and glossy, and had been expertly cut since she last saw him. Unlike hers, it curled only at the tips. Also he was taller than any other man in sight, which was a huge point in his favour on a day when she'd chosen to wear boots with four-inch heels.

'Is it difficult today?' asked Jonas, eyeing the blank crossword as he sat down beside her.

'I'm not in the mood.'

'You're still angry with me,' he observed.

'Not still. Again,' she corrected.

'Because I didn't ring before I arrived?'

'In the circumstances, yes,' she said, and drank some of the water he'd poured for her.

'I tried. You were on the phone. I left a message,' he informed her succinctly. 'Did you check?'

Avery flushed guiltily.

'You've obviously had a busy, stressful morning,' he said kindly, like a parent to a fractious child.

'Which doesn't excuse my bad manners. Sorry!' She gave him a rueful smile. 'Have you inspected the damage to Stow Street yet?'

'No. I came straight to you. You can walk me through the repairs you need before I drive you back.'

'Right.' She sighed. 'I know I'm lucky to have a business I can run from home, but I'll be glad to have the house to myself again.'

'Has the fire affected trade?'

'Not yet. We get a regular supply of work from the dress shop, and the main department store, and I travel to private homes for fittings—so that side of things shouldn't suffer. But I'll miss out on the jobs people pop in on their way into town from the car park.'

They were interrupted several times during lunch, by people sympathising about the fire, and Avery introduced Jonas each time, purposely omitting any qualifying description.

'I wasn't sure you'd want your official capacity broadcast to all and sundry,' she said in an undertone.

'It's not a problem,' he assured her, and gave her a look which brought her antennae erect. 'I don't mind who knows I represent Mercom—or the conclusions your friends jump to about our relationship, either. Just for the record,' he added, 'is there someone likely to resent me as a possible usurper?'

'No,' she said flatly, pouring coffee with a steady hand. 'I told you that early on in our brief acquaintance.'

'It still surprises me.'

'Why?'

Jonas leaned nearer, a look in his eyes which caused her considerable unrest. 'Because, Avery Crawford, I was attracted to you the first time I laid eyes on you—even in no-nonsense clothes with your hair scraped back.'

'And despite the fact that I was trying to pick you up?' she said, her voice tart to hide her pleasure.

'That too,' he admitted with a grin. 'But one look at you the following night, with that glorious hair loose and those lips painted red as sin, and I thought of gypsy violins—and sex.'

Avery put down her coffee cup with a bang and stood up. 'Time to go,' she said tersely.

Jonas got to his feet, smiling down at her. 'You look like Business Woman of the Year today, but my reaction's just the same.'

Avery waved at an acquaintance as they left the bar, then stalked across the courtyard with as much speed and dignity as her heels and the cobbles allowed. She was annoyed because secretly—she hoped it was secretly—his remarks had done serious damage to her self-possession.

They were on their way into town when he took his hand from the wheel for an instant to touch hers. 'Would you like to come down off your high horse and listen to Mercom's plans for the land I've purchased?'

She threw him an exasperated look. 'Of course I would.'

'The project's been brewing for a while, but until my recent visit I had never been here myself. I left the opening moves to others, while I was occupied with far bigger fish than providing a small market town with a cinema complex.'

Avery stared at him, eyes wide. 'A cinema? I thought you were building a warehouse.'

'It was the original intention. But after I'd had a look at the place myself I had a word with my father, then spoke to the local council and suggested something of use to the community.' Jonas turned into Stow Street and made for the car park. 'The necessary parking space is right here, and the nearest cinema is fifteen miles away.'

She smiled warmly. 'That's such a brilliant idea!'

'One I intended to share with you over dinner at the Walnut Tree that night. But circumstances conspired against me, one way and another,' he said wryly, and killed the engine.

Avery stared at him in remorse. 'I can't believe I forgot to ask. What happened about the accident?'

Jonas shrugged. 'It was messy, and put paid to one of our vehicles, but the driver escaped with a couple of fractures— one of them to his jaw. The culprit was a van which shot a red light, but by some miracle no one was killed.' His eyes met hers. 'I thought about ringing later that night, but in the end decided against it.'

Avery nodded morosely. 'I don't blame you. I was a total shrew.'

His lips twitched. 'You were very scary. So was that room. It reminded me of a painful interview in my headmaster's study after I was caught climbing into the wrong dormitory.'

'Was that such a hanging offence, then?'

'Pretty much. The dormitory was in the local girls' school.'

Avery gave a snort of laughter.

Jonas grinned. 'It wouldn't have been so bad if I'd been caught climbing out, but as it was I got all the flak and none of the fun. Rather like that last evening with you,' he added.

'I refuse to do any more apologising,' she said flatly as they walked towards her shop. 'Grovelling doesn't come easy to me.'

'I can tell! Just for the record, I would have liked to outline Mercom's plans that night at the Fleece, but at that stage certain people still had a few dotted lines to sign on.' He shot her a sidelong glance. 'You seemed angry out of all proportion to the circumstances. Why?'

Avery unlocked the shop, ushered him inside, and closed the door before she answered. 'When I was told Mercom had bought the land, and might demolish the shops in Stow Street for all I knew, I was hurt because you hadn't been straight with me. I met a lot of devious men in my time in the City.' She looked at him squarely. 'I thought you were different.'

Jonas held her eyes. 'I didn't ring you the moment I received confirmation because I wanted to hand you the letter in person and bask in your gratitude. It's a long time since that boy climbed up to a window to impress a girl, but it was the same motivation, Avery. So shall we start again?'

Start what? 'By all means,' she said lightly. 'It wouldn't do for me to upset my landlord.'

'True. I rather like the idea of having a hold over you,' he said with satisfaction, and then sobered abruptly as he inspected the shop and its half-gutted neighbour. 'A good thing there's an alley between this and the flower shop.'

'When I saw it my first reaction was to find new premises,' Avery admitted. 'The shop has always been too small for the services we offer, but the rent is reasonable and its location is good, so I'd rather stay if possible. What do you think of the damage to my place?'

'It looks superficial, but I'll have my people check it out right away. You'll probably want to use local tradesmen to redecorate, but Mercom will foot the bill. Get someone to do a rush job for you.'

Avery introduced Jonas to her fellow leaseholders, and looked on in amusement as the new landlord chatted easily with each one in turn.

He thanked her as they walked back to his car. 'Once I've driven you home I've got meetings with various people this afternoon, to tie up a few loose ends. I leave again first thing tomorrow, so have dinner with me tonight to celebrate the deal.'

Instead of jumping at the invitation Avery gave it some thought. In some ways it was good to live in a small town, where she was known to everyone, but in others—as in this instance—it was a drawback. Jonas Mercer's identity and his firm's plans for the land he'd bought would soon be common knowledge after his tour of inspection this afternoon. The jungle drums would go into overdrive if she was seen socialising with the head of Mercom for the second time in one day.

'A plain, honest-to-God no will do,' said Jonas dryly as he drove off.

She shook her head. 'I was about to say yes, but only if

I cook something at home. I like to keep a low social profile.'

'You're ashamed to be seen out with me,' he accused.

She shot him a kindling look. 'Do you want dinner at my place or not?'

'You know damn well I do. Order in and I'll foot the bill. There must be a Chinese or Indian in town?'

'Good idea. You're not just a pretty face after all,' she said in approval.

'That's you, Avery Crawford, not me.' He smiled. 'I'll be back here at eight. Sort out a decorator, and anything else you need, and let me know the details over dinner.'

Avery felt a lot more pleased with life as she went into her house to report that the new landlord was footing the bill to refurbish the premises in Stow Street and that cleaning up and painting could start right away. There were relieved smiles all round.

Once Helen and Louise had left for the day Frances demanded a detailed report on the working lunch with Jonas Mercer.

'I told him that when I saw the damage on Saturday night my first thought was new premises. Which is true enough. We could do with space for a proper fitting room.'

'But that would mean higher rent and a far less appealing landlord!'

Avery grinned. 'An inescapable truth, which decided me to stick with Stow Street.'

'So are relations more cordial now between you and Jonas?' asked Frances.

'Yes. We still have things to discuss, so I've asked him to dinner here tonight.'

'Have you, indeed? What's on the menu?'

'He suggested ordering in.'

Frances shook her head. 'Impress him with some home cooking. Men find that sexy.'

Avery's eyebrows rose. 'Was that your reaction when Philip cooked lunch for you yesterday?'

'Yes,' said her friend candidly. 'It's the first time a man has ever made a meal for me, and I loved it. Grill our new landlord a steak, or whatever, and he'll probably say yes to whatever you want,' she added, batting her eyelashes.

'In that case I'd better nip down to the shops as soon as we finish for the day.'

When she got back from her shopping trip Avery was touched to find Frances had stayed on to work magic with a duster and a vacuum cleaner.

'I've only done downstairs,' she warned.

'You shouldn't have done any of it. And downstairs is quite enough. He's only coming to dinner, Frances! But thanks a lot. You're an angel. Now I can get on with the meal. Not that there's much cooking involved. What do you think of rib-eye steak, green salad and roast potatoes?'

'Perfect. Straight to any man's heart. I might try it on Philip tomorrow.'

'You mean you're not seeing him tonight?'

'He wanted to.' Frances pulled on her coat, smiling wryly. 'But these days caution's my middle name, so I held out for Tuesday.'

Shortly before Jonas was due to arrive the roasting potatoes were scenting the air, the steaks were ready to grill, and the salad greens lacked only a splash of dressing.

Thanks to the hot steam in her shower, and more during her cooking, Avery's hair curled in wild profusion on her shoulders. She'd deliberately painted her lips the exact shade of her clinging crimson sweater, and for good measure she'd hung big gypsy hoops in her ears. But to make it clear that it was just a casual kitchen supper she wore jeans, and hadn't bothered with candles or one of her mother's table-cloths.

Jonas arrived a minute before the clock struck eight, and stood transfixed when Avery opened the door to him.

'Hi. You're on time,' she said, smiling.

'And you're a vision!' He handed her a bottle of wine and a great sheaf of tulips. 'Perfect. If I were an artist I'd paint you—just as you are right now.'

'Why, thank you. What gorgeous flowers. Come through to the kitchen so I can put them in water.'

Jonas followed her along the hall, sniffing the air. 'The food's here already? It was supposed to be my treat.'

'I thought I'd cook.' Avery put the flowers in the kitchen sink and bent to search in a cupboard for a vase, taking her time over it to let him enjoy her back view. She flipped her hair back as she straightened, and met a look in Jonas's eyes which brought heat to her face. 'What would you like to drink? I've got some red wine opened ready, or you can have a beer. Do sit down,' she added.

'Wine would be good,' he said. 'Can I pour one for you?'

'Yes, please.' She switched on the grill. 'How do you like your steak?'

'Medium rare.' Jonas filled two glasses and hooked out a chair, taking undisguised pleasure in watching her. 'This is a very good way to spend an evening,' he said, with such lazy satisfaction that Avery couldn't help smiling at him as she arranged the tulips in a fat blue jug. 'I had a chat with the manager of the hotel about the fire earlier on,' he went on. 'Apparently no one knows who was responsible.'

'Except me. I can identify one of the culprits.' Avery put the steaks to grill. She turned to face him. 'He stumbled under a streetlight as he ran after his chums. I saw his face clearly.'

'Did you, indeed?' Jonas's eyes narrowed. 'Are you going to do anything about it?'

'Are you asking as head of Mercom, or merely from curiosity?'

'Nothing you tell me will go any further, if that's the way you want to play it.'

'I do.' Avery eyed him in silence for a moment. 'For your ears only, his name is Daniel Morrell—son of George, our friendly local property developer.'

CHAPTER FOUR

JONAS gave a low whistle. 'Daddy wouldn't like that at all!'

'Daddy doesn't have to find out,' said Avery with emphasis. 'Daniel knows I spotted him, so I think the best punishment is to just let him stew, poor kid.'

'The ''poor kid'' was responsible for a fire,' Jonas reminded her.

'With George for a father, wouldn't you kick over the traces occasionally?'

'My traces never involved pyrotechnics.'

'Just girls, I suppose!'

'Mostly,' he admitted smugly.

'At least Dan's sins weren't intentional. It must have been a faulty rocket.'

'But he set it off in dangerous proximity to property— Mercom property,' Jonas added. 'But because you've told me in confidence I won't say a word—those steaks smell good.'

Avery spun round to check, and switched off the grill. She transferred the pan of potatoes from the oven and slid sizzling steaks onto warmed plates.

'No first course,' she said, pushing the salad bowl towards him. 'This is it, so help yourself and eat.'

The potatoes had been roasted to crisp perfection over unpeeled garlic cloves and sprigs of rosemary, and Jonas made relishing noises as he tasted them. 'Someone with looks like yours shouldn't cook like this, Avery.'

She eyed him warily. 'Why not?'

He smiled. 'It's not fair on a poor defenceless male.'

'If you answer to that description you're the first of the

species I've ever met! I took a chance on the garlic because I like it,' she added.

'The entire meal is perfect. Tell me, Avery Crawford,' he added, 'you're beautiful, successful, and you can even cook—so why—'

'Why hasn't some man snapped me up long since?' she finished, resigned.

His lips twitched. 'It's a subject that's obviously come up before. So why *are* you still single?'

Avery shrugged. 'The beauty is illusion—courtesy of my hair and a few cosmetics—and my business is successful because I concentrate all my energies on it, with no calls on my time from man or child. When I come home at night I please myself, instead of cooking meals and ironing shirts and so on.'

His eyebrows rose. 'Is that how you think of marriage?'

'I'm self-supporting and I own my own home, so I don't think of it at all.'

'Love and companionship usually come into it somewhere.'

She shook her head. 'Too much of a gamble. Past relationships promised both, and in the end failed on all counts. But with no marriage lines to cloud the issue I was able to walk away each time.'

'With no regrets?'

Her eyes fell. 'Oh, yes. There were plenty of those.'

Jonas looked at her downcast face for a moment, then laid down his knife and fork. 'That was the best meal I've ever eaten,' he informed her.

'Thank you, kind sir.' Avery bobbed a mock curtsy as she got up to collect their plates. 'But you liked the meal at the Fleece, surely?'

He shook his head. 'No restaurant food can compare with a meal enjoyed in the company of the beautiful woman who cooked it.'

Amused by the smooth flattery, Avery got busy with coffee. 'No pudding, I'm afraid.' She handed him the tray. 'Would you bring it into the other room, please?'

'If you mean that deep freeze of a drawing room, I'd rather stay here in this nice warm kitchen,' Jonas said bluntly.

She smiled mysteriously, and beckoned him along the hall to a door near the foot of the stairs. '"Come into my parlour," said the spider to the fly.'

The small book-lined room was comfortably shabby, with French windows hung with tawny velvet curtains. Other than a desk with a computer, the only piece of furniture was a sofa drawn up to a log fire crackling behind a screen made of pierced brass petals. 'My study,' she announced, and put another log on the fire. 'Those windows look out on the back garden.'

Jonas put the tray down on the desk and looked around in approval. 'Now, this I like.'

Her face shadowed. 'This was my mother's retreat when she came back home to live after my father died.'

He gave her a searching look as he took the coffee she poured for him. 'You haven't mentioned your father before.'

Avery took the other corner of the sofa. Her first instinct was to change the subject, as usual. But for once she found that she wanted to talk about her father. And it was supposed to be easier to confide in strangers. Not that Jonas felt like a stranger any more.

'John Avery was a policeman,' she told him. 'My mother met him just as she finished training in London. It was love at first sight, and a baby on the way soon afterwards. They arranged a quick register office ceremony in Bermondsey, but two days before the wedding my father was fatally injured during an arrest. So Ellen Crawford had to return to her home town in the role of unmarried mother. They didn't have single parents in those days.' Avery smiled sardonically. 'It may sound like pure soap opera to you, but thirty years ago that kind of thing still mattered in a small town like this, where everyone knows everyone else.'

'Did it matter to you?'

'Only because it did to my mother and my grandparents. So to give them something to be proud of I worked my socks off to stay top of the class right through school.' She shrugged. 'The same motivation kept me here after my mother died instead of hotfooting it back to the City. By making Avery Alterations a success I'm thumbing my nose at certain people with long memories.'

'How about your father's family?'

'My mother used to take me to Bermondsey to see them when I was young, but they died when I was in primary school.' Avery smiled at him. 'There. You know things about me I've never told anyone else. You're a good listener, Jonas Mercer. Maybe you should have been a priest.'

He shook his head emphatically. 'Not the life for me.'

'No sex, you mean?'

He laughed. 'Sadly no vocation either!' He paused, eyeing her thoughtfully. 'If you've never spoken about your father before, Avery, your past relationships can't have been very close. I assume one of them involved Paul Morrell?'

She nodded. 'We knew each other by sight as children, but oddly enough we met as adults for the first time in London through friends. As I mentioned before, his parents didn't like that at all.'

'Why?'

Avery smiled cynically. 'When my grandmother died, shortly after my grandfather, my mother inherited the house, but there was so little cash to go with it that she took in all the dressmaking jobs she could get to support us. Paul's mother was a regular customer, and I was the one who delivered the finished garments to her. One way and another,

I don't make it to the Morrells' social list.' She got up to refill their cups. 'Would you like some brandy with this?'

'No, thanks.' Jonas stretched out his legs comfortably. 'I have everything a man could ask for right now.' He turned his head to look at her. 'I won't ask for more just yet.'

'Are you the kind of man who asks?'

'Always,' he said piously. 'My mother taught me to say please and thank you and always see old ladies across the road.'

'Whether they want to cross or not?'

He grinned. 'What I'm trying to say, Avery Crawford, is that however much I may lust for you I won't act on it until you want me to.'

She eyed him curiously. 'You're certain I will at some stage, then?'

'Positive.'

'So Frances was right.'

Jonas shot her a narrowed look. 'About what?'

'She says men find cooking sexy. I can't base that on personal experience, because my past relationships were in London, where meals are just a phone call away. Not,' Avery added hastily, 'that *this* is a relationship.'

'I am your landlord,' he pointed out. 'You lease property from me. So in my book that's definitely a relationship. Who knows? It may grow closer with time. I can wait.'

She smiled. 'You don't climb through bedroom windows any more, you mean?'

He laid his hand on his heart. 'If it meant open arms greeting me in yours I'd be happy to risk life and limb!'

Avery shook her head, amused. 'I'd want to know a whole lot more about a man before I got to that stage.'

'My life is an open book,' he assured her. 'With me, Avery Crawford, what you see is what you get.'

'Not all the time! You were pretty secretive about taking over as my new landlord.'

'As I've said before, I had to wait until it was official.' He sighed. 'I'd hoped you'd smother me with gratitude, but all I got for my pains was a ticking off. Twice, if we count this morning.'

Avery's colour rose. 'I've said I'm sorry, and I've cooked dinner for you. That's as grateful as I get. Smothering isn't my style.'

'I'm about to make you an offer which might change your mind.' Jonas laughed at the look she threw at him. 'You're not very big on trust, Ms Crawford.'

'Maybe not, but I'm *very* big on curiosity. What do you have in mind?'

'The betting chain has decided to move on, so once the repairs are done how do you feel about expanding Avery Alterations to include their old premises?'

'What a great idea!' She paused, eyeing him suspiciously. 'Is this the part where I smother you with gratitude?'

Jonas shrugged. 'It's not mandatory. You can have the premises—at a slightly higher rent than before, naturally— with no strings attached.'

His eyes held hers for a long, charged moment, and suddenly Avery felt impatient with her own hypocrisy. She had broken her own rules by inviting Jonas to dinner here, and had dressed very deliberately to entice—not only in the clinging crimson sweater but in the matching bits of lace worn underneath it. And he'd made it clear she would have to make the first move.

Before she could change her mind she leaned forward until her lips rested on his. Jonas tensed for an instant, then caught her in his arms, kissing her with a controlled, banked-down heat she could actually feel rising up inside him, like mercury in a thermometer. Her body flushed with answering warmth as his hands slid under her sweater, and she kissed him back with such fervour that she felt his shoulder muscles knot under her hands, warning her that any minute now Jonas would want to take her to bed.

If he'd been waiting for her to lust for him in equal measure she was sending out all the right signals—every last one of them. He pulled her onto his lap and she felt his erection already hard under her thighs, as his lips and tongue and caressing hands brought her to the point where she was almost ready to do anything he wanted—but not quite.

Abruptly Avery broke free and backed into her corner of the sofa. Jonas sat very still, jaw clenched. Their laboured breathing was so loud in the tense silence that Avery jumped out of her skin when a log crashed from the fire and sparks flew up. She got up, surprised that her legs were willing to support her. She added more logs, fiddled with the fire, and played for time by brushing the hearth. But at last she turned to find Jonas on his feet, arms outstretched, and without hesitation she walked into their embrace.

'Why did you change your mind, Avery?'

'You'll laugh if I tell you.'

He smoothed the tumbled curls back from her forehead. 'Try me.'

She leaned closer, her voice muffled against his shoulder. 'I've lived a very low-key life since I came back here. Socially, you're the only man to make it through my door— let alone into my bedroom.'

He tipped her face up to his. 'Then why did you ask me back that first night?'

'I trusted my instincts. I was sure you wouldn't misunderstand the invitation.'

'I didn't at the time, but we got our wires badly crossed just now,' he said ruefully.

'Not really.' She met his eyes squarely. 'As once before in our short acquaintance, Mr Mercer, I was the one who started it.'

'Why did you stop?'

Her eyes fell. 'I'm out of practice at this kind of thing. I suddenly got cold feet. Besides, my bedroom's a disaster area and the bathroom's even worse— It may sound silly,' she said crossly, as he threw back his head and laughed, 'but you did ask.'

Jonas drew her down on the sofa beside him and took her hand. 'Avery, there isn't a man alive who would care a damn about your bedroom so long as it had a bed and he could make love to you in it. And it wouldn't have to be a bed, or even a bedroom. The floor right here would do.'

'A bit dangerous with a log fire!'

'True. And since the last thing I need right now is added heat we'll keep to the sofa and talk.' He lifted her hand to his lips, his eyes utterly serious. 'First, there are one or two things you need to know.'

Avery's heart sank. 'Don't tell me—you're married.'

'For God's sake,' he snapped, flinging her hand away. 'That's a damned offensive remark, Avery Crawford. If I had a wife this situation would never have arisen.'

'All right, all right,' she said hastily. 'I apologise—again. What were you going to confess?'

'Explain, not confess.'

Avery moved away to curl up in the other corner of the sofa. 'So explain.'

'A plate on my office door back at base reads "Deputy Chief Executive". This rather grand title means that normally I wouldn't be involved in a small undertaking like the cinema complex here. Mercom employs other people to do that.'

'So why are you here?'

He shrugged. 'My father handed over his responsibilities a damn sight too soon for my liking. Don't get me wrong— I enjoy what I do. But sometimes I get the urge to go walk-about. This particular project came up during one of my restless spells, so I insisted on coming myself.' He smiled crookedly. 'But I was bored rigid that first evening at the Angel, cursing myself for not sending someone else. Then a beautiful woman asked to share my table...'

'I looked anything but beautiful,' she said dryly. 'I was trying to fade into the background, remember?'

'Impossible the way you look now!' He eyed her flushed face and tumbled hair. 'There were raised eyebrows when I said I was coming here again today. Someone else was supposed to inspect the fire damage and sort everything, including the offer of extra premises.'

'So why did you come?'

His eyes held hers. 'You know the answer to that. I wanted to see you again, to make sure everything was done for you that could be done. But it took some juggling to get away, and I may not make it back here again for a while.'

'I realise that.'

Jonas pulled her back onto his lap and looked down into her eyes. 'But I will be back—believe me. So in the meantime don't get any other man's hopes up, Avery. We started something tonight, and sooner rather than later I intend to go on with it.' He kissed her, sliding his hands through her hair to hold her still.

Her heart raced as his tongue slid between her lips, and suddenly it was simple. She murmured something and he raised his head in disbelief.

'What did you say?'

'Let's go on with it now.'

He leapt up, pulling her to her feet to rush her to the door, and Avery gave a husky, breathless little laugh to hide nerves which were back in full force. Idiotic! One didn't forget how to make love.

Jonas paused outside in the hall to kiss her very thoroughly, then gave her a little push towards the stairs. Heart thumping, Avery hurried up ahead of him to open her bedroom door.

'At least the bed is made,' she said huskily, kicking off her shoes, and he laughed and swung her up in his arms to lay her against the pillows.

'I like a woman with the right priorities,' he said as he hung over her. 'Darling, you're shivering.'

'Stage fright,' she said gruffly. 'It's been a long time.'

He dropped a kiss on her lips, then stretched out beside her and took her in his arms, rubbing his cheek against hers. 'You'll soon pick it up again. It's like riding a bike.'

She gave an unsteady little chuckle. 'And they said romance was dead!'

Jonas stroked a finger down her cheek. 'You don't have to do this, Avery.'

'Do you want to?'

'What kind of damn fool question is that?'

He held her hand against his erection as tangible proof, but touching him was no antidote to her shivering. I am a grown woman, she told herself. I have done this before. But this time, with this man, she knew beyond doubt it would be different.

Jonas turned her in his arms. And as she smiled into the intent, searching eyes Avery relaxed, her nerves suddenly gone. 'I do too,' she whispered.

He traced the curve of her parted mouth with the tip of his tongue and bit gently on the bottom lip. Then kissed it better, and went on kissing her until they were both breathing raggedly. He sat up to strip off his shirt, and slid to his feet to get rid of the rest, but when Avery rolled away to take off her sweater he dived across the bed.

'No. This part is mine.'

He pulled her back against him, his hands roving under her sweater as he whispered a question into the nape of her neck. Avery shook her head and pushed her bottom hard against him. Jonas growled and flipped her over on her back, taking her sweater over her head almost in the same movement. He peeled her bra away, and bent his head to graze his mouth over her breasts, but she tensed as he undid her jeans.

'I've got a scar,' she said huskily.

He slid the jeans away and looked down at the line of red above the remaining triangle of lace. Very gently he put his lips to it, and she shivered as he dispensed with the lace to bury his face against her satiny warmth. Avery felt his hair brush against her skin and arched like a bow as his invading, caressing fingers sent waves of sensation rushing through her body. Jonas surged up to cover her, his hands fisted in her tumbled mass of hair as he crushed her mouth with devouring kisses which she returned feverishly, her thighs parted in urgent welcome to the entire velvet length of him as he thrust hard and deep inside her.

Her eyes snapped shut, but he growled, 'Look at me!' and she obeyed, her eyes locked with his as their bodies moved in urgent rhythm. Her breath tore through her chest, her hair tossed back and forth on the pillows and her hips ground against his, flesh on flesh, as they surged together in such frenzy it took superhuman effort for Jonas to hold himself back until she gasped, arching against him in climax. Then he buried his face in her hair, abandoning himself to the same engulfing pleasure.

Afterwards, still held close in his arms, Avery realised why making love with Jonas Mercer had been different from anything experienced before. In the past some part of her had always been looking on, watching the proceedings with a kind of detached amusement that she was involved in something so outrageously intimate. But with Jonas all conscious thought had been blotted out—right from ravishing beginning to heart-stopping, orgasmic end.

At last Avery stirred a little, and Jonas rolled on his back, holding her prone on top of him as he drew the covers up. 'You see? You hadn't forgotten.'

'No.' She smiled down into his eyes and stretched against him. 'But it was nothing like riding a bike.'

'Is that a compliment?'

'If you want marks out of ten—eleven, at least,' she assured him.

Jonas brought her head down to his and kissed her very thoroughly. 'A man likes to know he's appreciated.'

Avery sighed as she turned to look at the clock. 'You'd better go, or you might get locked out at the Fleece.'

He shook his head smugly, his hands tightening on her hips. 'I'm in the annexe at the back. Or do you want me to go now you've had your wicked way with me?'

She tapped him on the nose, laughing. 'Is that what I've done?'

'What do you do on weekends?'

Avery blinked at the abrupt change of subject. 'I man the shop alone on Saturdays, and Sundays I do my chores.' She looked over her shoulder at the underwear spilling from half closed drawers, and the chaos on her dressing table. 'Much needed ones,' she said with a shudder.

'Was it really just your housekeeping that made you put on the brakes downstairs?'

'Not entirely.' Her eyes fell. 'My scar was part of it, too.'

'Were you afraid I'd hurt you?'

'No. I thought it might put you off,' she said, flushing.

'You soon discovered your mistake,' he said, in a tone which sent delicious shivers down the naked spine he was caressing. 'I want to see you again. Soon. Would your friend take over for you if you have a Saturday off?'

'Probably,' she said, pleased he'd changed the subject.

'I'll make sure I'm free the weekend after next. Does that work for you?'

'Yes,' she said doubtfully. 'But—'

'But you'd rather not socialise with me on your home turf?'

She nodded ruefully. 'It was sheer bravado on my part to say I might not be free when you come, because I go to most events in the town alone or with Frances. The few—very few—eligible men around here gave up on me long ago.'

Jonas twined a lock of her hair round a finger. 'So if you were seen with me on a regular basis it would be taken for granted that I'm your lover,' he said with satisfaction.

'You bet it would. And if you were anyone else that wouldn't matter in the slightest. We're both free agents. But you're the man from Mercom and my landlord, and you're even going to let me have extra premises. I've worked too hard to make Avery Alterations a success to risk gossip that could be bad for business.'

'Why should there be gossip?' he said, surprised.

'It's the lifeblood of a small town like this.'

'Then run away with me to the country.'

'I'd love to, but I don't even know where you live.'

'I bought a house last year in the green depths of Herefordshire.'

'That's a long haul for a commute!'

'My main home is in London. The country place is a weekend retreat, but I haven't retreated there very often lately.' Jonas held her closer. 'I could get there the weekend after next. So come with me. Or meet me there.'

Avery liked the idea a lot. 'All right, I will. But just as an experiment. We might be at each other's throats by the time we leave.'

'I seriously doubt that! Come in time for Saturday lunch, and stay over Sunday night.' He smiled into her eyes as he flattened his hand at the base of her spine, and heat rushed through Avery as she found he was ready to make love again. 'But that's two weeks away,' he said, as he brought her mouth down to his. 'Let's concentrate on the here and now.'

CHAPTER FIVE

'SOMETHING very erotic about sneaking out of your house in the small hours,' Jonas whispered when he finally kissed her goodbye. 'I'll ring you tonight.'

Avery staggered out of bed after only a couple of hours' sleep, stood under the shower until she woke up a little, then reluctantly set to work. The kitchen had to be immaculate and all signs of her turbulent night erased from both bedroom and bathroom before she could get dressed and slap on some war paint.

'You look a bit tired this morning, boss.' Frances, always the first to arrive, smiled conspiratorially. 'So how did it go? Did our new landlord enjoy his taste of home cooking?'

'He certainly did.' Avery flushed as she met a knowing blue eye.

'So the evening was a success?'

'Yes.'

'Are you seeing him again?'

'He's going back this morning.'

'That's not what I asked.'

Avery held up her hands in surrender. 'All right, all right. I'm seeing him the weekend after next—but only if you'll do my Saturday for me.'

'Of course I will,' said Frances impatiently. 'Is he coming back here?'

'No. I'm meeting him at his weekend cottage.'

'Are you, indeed? Where is it?'

'I'm not sure, exactly—somewhere in Herefordshire.'

The arrival of the others put an end to further catechism. The phone started ringing and Avery Alterations—temporary relocation or not—was up and running on a normal working day.

Avery spent part of it in the car, driving to fittings, but on the way back she went to Stow Street to meet the owner of a firm of builders she'd used in the past—one of a list of tradesmen she'd given Jonas. She was impressed to find that Frank Crowley had already received instructions from Mercom to submit an estimate for the alterations required, and after some in-depth discussion with him on the renovation she left for Gresham Road, reassured that with Mercom—and Jonas—in the driving seat Avery Alterations would soon be back in town.

Avery smiled in triumph as she showed her team a rough sketch of the plans for the new premises. 'Complete with a fair-sized fitting room, plus space for me to do my restoration jobs on site, instead of here at home.'

'Brilliant. How long will it take, boss?' asked Helen, impressed.

'According to Frank Crowley we should be in fairly soon. The Mercom name worked like a charm.'

'God bless them!' Louise beamed. 'I love the idea of a cinema. No more driving for miles to take my little dears to watch the latest Disney offering.'

'Talking of little dears,' said Avery, tapping her watch. 'Time you two were off.'

'I assume Jonas is wielding the magic wand?' said Frances after they'd gone.

'Yes.' Avery shot her a look. 'But I'd rather no one knows I'm seeing him socially.'

'I shan't say a word.' Frances crossed her heart. 'Not even to Philip.'

'Thank you.' Avery smiled wryly. 'As I told Jonas, the local grapevine would probably say I'd acquired the new premises by sleeping with my landlord. According to some

I only wangled the lease in the first place by sleeping with Paul Morrell.'

'Look on the bright side,' said Frances, rinsing cups. 'They could have said you wangled it by sleeping with his father!'

Later, after Frances had left to keep her date with Philip Lester, Avery took her coffee into the study after supper, intending to tackle some paperwork when she found the energy. Ignoring the computer, she curled up on the sofa, knowing that before she could settle to any work she needed to hear from Jonas.

This was a bit worrying. Their night together had been wonderful, and the lovemaking so sublime she shivered every time she thought of it. But falling in love with him— or any other man—was not on her agenda. She'd been there, done that, and had no intention of risking the same kind of heartache again.

But when she answered her phone her heart leapt at the sound of Jonas Mercer's deep, lazy tones.

'How are things with you this evening, Avery?'

'Fair. And you?'

'Weary. The motorway was practically gridlocked at one stage on my drive to London, which left me in no mood for a day of endless meetings.' He chuckled. 'My obvious fatigue won me a suggestion that in future I delegate tiring routine trips to those I employ to take care of them.'

'How did you respond to that?'

'I drew myself up to my full height—always a good move—and informed the speaker and everyone else in earshot that if I feel the need to oversee any project personally I shall do so whenever I think fit.'

'Very masterful! Did he shrivel?'

'You bet. People will be treading very warily in my vicinity tomorrow.'

'Despot!'

'No harm in the occasional crack of the whip. My father was deeply impressed. Now, tell me your news. Did you meet your builder?'

'I certainly did. The Mercom name kick-started Frank Crowley into instant action. He's obviously after future work for you.'

'A strong possibility if he comes up to scratch. Tell him to send his estimate asap.'

'It's on its way as we speak. Ditto from his brother-in-law, the electrician.'

Jonas laughed. 'Nothing like keeping it in the family. What are you doing right now?' he added.

'Considering an early night.' She chuckled. 'You should do the same. Otherwise you might alienate your entire work-force tomorrow.'

'My workforce is not on my mind right now, Avery.' His voice deepened to an intimacy that quickened her pulse. 'Last night was such a ravishing experience it's going to seem like a very long time until our weekend together. Not that I shall rush you to bed the moment you set foot in my house,' he assured her.

A thrill ran down her spine at the thought. 'You mean you'll let me cook dinner first, I suppose? But I can't actually set foot in your house until you tell me where it is.'

'True. Pay attention.'

Avery took down lengthy instructions on how to find Jonas Mercer's retreat, surprised to find that for her it would be little more than an hour's drive. 'Why did you choose a place in that part of the world?' she asked.

'Friends of mine live in the area. They told me about the place, I fell in love at first sight, and now it's mine. You'll like it.'

She probably would, too, thought Avery later, as she switched on her computer. But if she had any sense she would steer clear of Jonas Mercer and his country cottage before she fell hopelessly in love with both of them.

She shrugged irritably. She was an adult with a brain, so surely it was possible to enjoy an affair with a man, even a man like Jonas, without letting her emotions get too deeply involved. For the past three years, purely from choice, there had been no man in her life. But now Jonas Mercer had come on the scene he would leave a big hole in that nice tidy life if she kept to her rule and excluded him from it. Besides, she liked the idea of a secret lover. It was the perfect arrangement. A stolen weekend now and again was far more appealing than the hassle of living together on a daily basis.

Next morning Avery was working alone in her spare room when Frances came in to say she was wanted downstairs.

'Who is it?'

'Mrs Morrell,' said Frances, rolling her eyes.

Avery scowled. 'What on earth does she want?'

'She wouldn't tell me, so I put her in the drawing room to wait. It's horribly cold in there, but I didn't think you'd want her in your study.'

'You thought right. Tell her I'll be down in a minute.' Avery went into her bedroom to find a lipstick that matched her pink sweater. She tucked a couple of stray curls into her knot of hair, shrugged into her jacket and replaced flat loafers with her tall-heeled black boots before going down to confront a woman she disliked for more reasons than Frances knew.

When Avery turned the big white porcelain knob on the drawing room door her visitor, short, dumpy and expensively dressed, eyed her apprehensively.

'Good morning,' said Avery, coolly polite. 'What can I do for you, Mrs Morrell?'

'Good morning. I know I should have rung first,' said the

woman stiffly, 'but I thought you might refuse to see me if I did.'

'Why should I do that?' Avery waved a hand towards one of the brocade chairs. 'Won't you sit down?'

'No, thanks. I won't take up much of your time. I'm here about Daniel.'

'Your son? What is Daniel to do with me, exactly?'

'You know perfectly well,' said Mrs Morrell with sudden passion. 'He's been in such a state lately I thought he was ill, but in the end he broke down and told me you saw him running away from the fire in Stow Street.'

Avery said nothing.

'There were other boys with Daniel. It isn't fair that he should get all the blame,' said his mother in anguish. 'I must know whether you intend to report him.'

'And if I do?'

'Tell me how much it would cost for you to change your mind.'

The words hung like icicles in the cold air of the room.

'You actually came to *bribe* me?' said Avery in disbelief.

'If you must put it like that.'

'What other way is there?'

Daphne Morrell opened her handbag and took out a chequebook. 'Name your price.'

'So you've come to buy me off. Does your husband know about this?' Avery eyed her coldly. 'Or maybe it was his idea, and he thought you might have better luck at playing on my sympathy.'

'Certainly not! He must never know I came here.' Painful colour rose in the other woman's face. 'Please, Miss Crawford, I beg you. Daniel's a good boy. I can't bear the thought of him in court. If you were a mother you'd understand.'

Avery's lips tightened. She looked down at her visitor in

stony silence for a moment, then turned on her heel and walked to the door. 'Put your chequebook away, Mrs Morrell. I'm very busy, so I must ask you to leave now.'

The woman's eyes filled with misery. 'You're really going to report Daniel to the police, then? Is it because I disapproved of your relationship with Paul?'

'No.' Avery's eyes hardened. 'But cast your mind back a few years to when I was Daniel's age, Mrs Morrell. In those days you weren't nearly so ready with your chequebook when I delivered the garments my mother had copied so expertly from *Vogue*, or whatever. You kept her waiting weeks for payment every time.'

The woman flinched, her face suddenly ashen. 'So this is your revenge?'

'Certainly not. I don't believe in suffering the sins of the mother on the child.'

Colour rushed back into the pallid face. 'Oh, thank God! I'm truly grateful. I can't tell you—'

'Not so fast, Mrs Morrell,' said Avery crisply. 'Before I let Daniel off I want a little chat with him. Tell him to come and see me.'

'I fail to see why that's necessary!' said the other woman, bristling, then met the look in Avery's eyes and capitulated hastily. 'Oh, very well.'

'Tell Daniel to come here at six this evening—on his own, please.'

Daphne Morrell paused in the hall on her way out, looking up at Avery in wonder. 'Your mother was such a small, gentle woman. You don't resemble her at all.'

'I take after my father. He was in the Metropolitan Police,' said Avery with pride. 'My resemblance to him was an enduring comfort to my mother. Good morning, Mrs Morrell.'

*　　*　　*

Daniel Morrell was a dark, good-looking youth, so much like his brother Avery felt a pang of adverse reaction as she opened the door to him that evening.

'Hi, I'm Dan Morrell. My mother said you wanted to see me, Miss Crawford.' He cracked his knuckles, then flushed hectically and put his hands behind his back.

So he was nervous—excellent.

'Good evening,' said Avery formally. 'Come in.'

She had intended taking the boy into the drawing room, but he looked so apprehensive she motioned him into the less daunting atmosphere of the study. 'Sit down, please.'

Dan perched on the edge of the sofa, but Avery stood erect in front of the fireplace, taking a leaf out of Jonas's book and using her height to intimidate.

'Right, then,' she said briskly. 'Were you the one who threw the rocket in Stow Street on Bonfire Night?'

'It was an accident, Miss Crawford. No one threw it.' He looked up at her in appeal. 'A crowd of us clubbed together to buy some fireworks to take to a party at my friend's house after the display in the park, but his father wouldn't let us fire them off in his garden and we couldn't think of any-where else—'

'So you let them off behind the shops instead?'

'We were as far away from them as possible—honestly, Miss Crawford. We couldn't do it near any houses, or in the park, so the building plot between the pub and the shops was the only place we could think of.' He thrust an agitated hand through his hair. 'We took all the necessary safety precautions, I swear, but that one rocket must have been defective.'

'So you ran away?'

He jumped to his feet, his face crimson again. 'I'm not proud of that. But I reported the fire on my mobile while we were legging it.'

'Something in your favour, I suppose.' Avery looked at

him thoughtfully. 'I told your mother that I wouldn't report you, Dan, because I don't believe in scapegoats. If there were others involved it's only fair they should take some of the blame.'

'They all wanted to,' he said urgently, 'but I was the idiot who tripped right under a streetlight. You identified me, so it's only right I carry the can.'

'Highly commendable. How many of you were there?'

'Three others besides me,' he said reluctantly.

'I see.' Avery looked at him in silence, which had the boy fidgeting uneasily by the time she spoke. 'Right then, D'Artagnan, you're obviously determined to let the Three Musketeers go free, so I'll respect that. You know your Dumas?'

'Not the book, but I've seen the film,' he said with a grin, then sobered abruptly. 'So what happens now?'

'Come back tomorrow at six, and I'll let you know what I've decided.'

When Jonas rang later he told Avery that even if she'd released him from his promise reporting Daniel Morrell to the police would have been a bad public relations move for Mercom. 'But you can still do it if you want to, Avery.'

'I don't, because he wasn't the only one involved. In the end I told young Dan to come back again tomorrow to learn his fate.' Avery chuckled. 'I won't report him, but I don't see why he should get off scot-free. He can do some gardening for me.'

'Good idea!'

'What kind of punishment did you get for the girls' dormitory crime?'

'Brutal. I was gated for a month.'

'How sad. Did the object of your passion wait patiently until you were free?'

'Did she hell! The fickle jade transferred her attentions to my best friend.'

'Oh, bad luck! Were you shattered?'

'Heartbroken. I was really fond of Charlie.'

Avery gave a snort of laughter. 'I walked into that one!'

They talked for a while longer, but at last Jonas told her he had a call on another line. 'I've got a very dull business dinner tomorrow night, but I'll ring you when I get home.'

'You don't have to.'

'I do, you know. Goodnight, darling.'

'Goodnight,' she said huskily, and took in a deep, shaky breath as she put the phone back.

Fool! She'd been called darling countless times before in her life. But never in a voice like Jonas Mercer's, which turned her knees and other less visible parts to jelly.

Avery was in bed the following night, trying hard to read, when Jonas finally rang.

'Did I wake you, Avery?'

'No. I was counting the minutes until I heard from you,' she assured him, flippant to disguise the simple truth.

'I wish I could believe that.'

Avery asked him about his day, but Jonas flatly refused to discuss it.

'*I* see. You're the type of man who doesn't like a woman to worry her pretty little head about such things,' she accused.

'It would be a brave man who could say that to *your* face, Avery Crawford—'

'I'm not pretty enough?' she pounced.

He groaned. 'I'm in a no-win situation here. If you must know, my day involved interminable meetings, followed by a dinner with interminable speeches. Are you satisfied?'

'Yes.'

'Good. Now, tell me about the arsonist. How did he react when you sentenced him to hard labour?'

Avery chuckled evilly as she described Daniel Morrell's face when she'd stated that she felt compensation was necessary for the disruption her business had suffered. 'At first he was limp with relief because I had no intention of reporting him. Then he went pea-green at the thought of asking his father to cough up financial compensation.'

Jonas laughed. 'I wish I'd been a fly on the wall.'

'When I said I had labour rather than money in mind, his relief was enormous. So on Sunday morning I shall have a willing, strapping lad working like a beaver in my garden.'

'Don't let him in the house!'

'Why not?'

'Teenage males are hormones on legs at that age.'

'I'm a bit mature for young Dan's taste, surely!'

'The lure of the sexy older woman is irresistible,' he assured her.

'Speaking from experience again?' she asked sweetly.

'Absolutely. At one time I burned with unrequited passion for my housemaster's wife.'

'Before or after you were lusting for the belle of the local girls' school?'

'Concurrently—I had hormones to spare at that age. So scrape your hair back and leave off the lipstick and perfume.'

'Anything else?' she said, laughing.

'No. I'll ring you tomorrow. Goodnight, darling.'

Jonas rang her as regularly as the demands of his life allowed, but she never knew exactly when. Instead of waiting in for his call, one evening she had to force herself to attend one of the events that crowded the town's winter calendar. A message on her answering machine when she came home was no substitute for actually speaking to Jonas. The sex was to blame, she told herself. After three years of abstinence it was affecting her brain.

After a lonely Saturday evening in front of a video, forewarned that there would be no phone call from Jonas, Avery got up early, ready to greet her slave labour when he arrived.

To her amusement Daniel arrived early, attired in hiking gear.

'Good morning, Miss Crawford,' he said, smiling eagerly. 'My mother doesn't want my father to know I'm here, so I couldn't bring any gardening tools.'

'Not to worry, I've got all the usual things.' Avery fetched a key and conducted him down the path to the garden shed. 'Do you need instructions? Or do you do any gardening at home?'

'I help my father sometimes, so I know what I'm doing,' he said, and grinned. 'Unless you want decking and a water feature.'

'Nothing so fancy,' she said, laughing. 'The laurel hedges need trimming—but only with secateurs or clippers, please. No machinery. If you have time there's some tidying to do in the herbaceous borders afterwards. I'll provide coffee at ten, and you can finish in time to get home for Sunday lunch. Fair?'

'I can work a lot later than that,' offered Dan instantly. 'We eat at night.'

Avery shook her head. 'Thanks just the same, but I blow the whistle at twelve-thirty; no overtime required.'

To keep an eye on her young gardener Avery took some sewing up to her bedroom and watched from her window as Dan set to with a will in the back garden. He really did know what he was doing, she noted with approval.

Ignoring Jonas's warning, Avery called Dan in for a break, as promised. He shed his muddy boots at the door, washed his hands at the sink, and downed several biscuits with his coffee at the kitchen table, plainly feeling much easier in her company after his labours. The moment he'd finished he thanked Avery, pulled on his boots, and went out into the garden to resume his labours.

When Avery called a final halt at the end of the morning Dan offered his services for the following Sunday.

'I didn't do half as much as I'd hoped today,' he said apologetically.

'I didn't expect you to. You've done marvels and I'm grateful,' Avery told him. 'But no further labour required. I won't be here next Sunday,' she added, smiling.

Next weekend she would be with Jonas.

CHAPTER SIX

AVERY set out on the following Saturday morning in tearing spirits, feeling like a teenager with a first crush at the prospect of seeing Jonas again.

Once the fast major road was behind her the route took her along winding minor roads, with views of rolling landscape and green Herefordshire fields which gleamed in the frosty sunlight which had replaced the wind and rain of the day before. She sang along with the radio as she drove at a leisurely pace, happy to take time to look at the scenery rather than get from A to B in a hurry. She was longing to see Jonas but she had no intention of arriving at the cottage too early, just the same. She wanted him there before her, waiting impatiently, with a fire blazing in what was sure to be a big fireplace—maybe an inglenook, if the cottage was old. Jonas had said very little about it, but she pictured his retreat as old and cosy, with beams and uneven floorboards, maybe even a four-poster bed.

At the thought of bed Avery's excitement intensified, and she came to the final landmark on the route. The village was pure picture-postcard, with an ancient church in the background, black and white half-timbered cottages, and a couple of inviting pubs lining the main street. At any other time she would have lingered to explore, but she put on speed instead once she was out in open country again.

His house, Jonas had told her, was on private property near a lake, and a little further on she spotted the sign for Eardismont. She turned cautiously down a farm track and negotiated a couple of cattle grids en route, until a glint of water confirmed that she was on target. But as she drew nearer her eyebrows rose. The building by the lake was no half-timbered cottage. It was, or had been, a barn, and it obviously belonged to Jonas because he was waiting outside, hair blowing in the breeze and his face alight with a smile of welcome.

The moment Avery switched off the engine Jonas scooped her out of her seat, his mouth on hers before she could say a word.

'You're late,' he said, raising his head a fraction.

'I wanted you to be here first, waiting impatiently,' she said breathlessly, and kissed him back.

'You got your wish,' he growled, and kissed her again. 'Let's get your gear in the house and have lunch.'

'I want to explore this famous retreat of yours first!'

'That won't take long.' He took her velvet windbreaker, smiling at the look on her face when she crossed the threshold. The main room, which appeared to take up most of the ground floor space, was furnished with magnificent disregard for the building's origins. Plain natural linen hung at the tall windows and covered a pair of sofas large enough to suit someone of Jonas's dimensions. A square of glass supported on a marble plinth stood between them, topped by a mythical winged lion.

'Greek,' said Jonas, following her gaze. 'And that too,' he added, pointing to a side table which held a bronze helmet Agamemnon might have worn.

Instead of the inglenook fireplace of her imagining there was a square aperture on the far wall, with man-made flames dancing on a heap of pebbles, and slatted white cupboards in alcoves either side of it. A stone relief had been fixed to the wall above the fire, carved with cavalrymen from ancient Greece, but otherwise there wasn't a picture in sight.

Avery turned to Jonas in amazement. 'Is this your taste, or did you get an interior designer?'

'All my own work,' he assured her, and led her up a spiral

staircase to a vast bedroom with a raftered ceiling. But instead of a four-poster Jonas's bed was modern and big, flanked by side-tables with lamps, and facing a television on the far wall.

'Those doors over there lead to a dressing room and a bathroom, but there's only one bed.' He put her grip down, his eyes holding hers. 'If you don't fancy sharing I can take one of the sofas.'

'Do you snore?'

'I don't know. Do you?'

'I don't know, either.'

They looked at each other in silence for a moment longer, then they were in each other's arms, kissing with sudden, desperate craving, their hands clumsy in their haste to get each other naked. Jonas collapsed on the bed with Avery in his arms, rolling over to pin her down, his lips and tongue on her nipples in sucking caresses that made her so frantic her hand closed round him in a retaliating caress that put an abrupt end to foreplay. His mouth crushed hers and she clasped him with arms and legs as he thrust inside her, both of them overpowered by mutual need.

'I lied,' said Jonas a long time later.

Avery raised her head from his shoulder, her heavy eyes smiling into his. 'About what?'

'I said I wouldn't rush you to bed the minute you got here.'

'Am I complaining?' She raised herself up on one elbow and shook her dishevelled curls away from her face. 'Jonas, I've just thought of something.'

His eyes glittered between spiky lashes in the bright afternoon light. 'What is it?'

'You said something—quite some time ago, I might add—about lunch. But where's your kitchen?'

'Through a door under the staircase.'

'I was too stunned by the decor to notice it.'

He stroked a caressing hand over the smooth skin of her shoulder. 'My bits of antiquity need their space—like me.' He grinned. 'I'd suffer permanent concussion in one of those cottages in the village.'

An ominous rumble from Avery's midriff won a kiss from Jonas before he began pulling on his clothes. 'We need food.'

The galley-style kitchen was strictly functional, with just enough room for a table laid for lunch near a glass door leading into the garden.

'You sit and I'll get the meal—which is pretty basic,' Jonas warned, and pulled a chair out for her.

Avery was happy to obey. She felt pleasantly languorous, content to watch as Jonas put a basket of bread and a platter of cheese on the table. He filled bowls with steaming soup from an insulated jug and sat down, smiling indulgently as she snatched a piece of bread.

'I'm starving,' she said defensively. 'I was rather hoping for coffee when I arrived.'

'I intended to make some, but the blood left my brain the moment I set eyes on you,' he told her, and smiled into her eyes. 'It feels very, very good to have you here in my house, Avery Crawford.'

'It feels good to me, too.' She returned the smile luminously, and he reached out a hand to touch hers.

'You need to keep your strength up, so eat,' he ordered. 'I warn you now: I intend to make demands on your energy this weekend.'

Avery raised an eyebrow as she drank some soup. 'Is a ten-mile hike on the programme?'

'Nothing so strenuous,' he assured her. 'After lunch I suggest a brisk little walk to make the most of the weather, then tea in front of whatever sport we can find on television. Not in bed,' he added, reading her mind. 'There's a television in one of the cupboards by the fire.'

After lunch Avery felt utterly happy as she walked in the crisp, cold sunshine with Jonas. While they skirted the lake they talked non-stop, catching up on any news left out of their telephone conversations. When they ventured further Jonas pointed out a large house, the roof just visible through the trees in the distance.

'My landlord's country seat,' said Jonas. 'He let me buy the barn, with the proviso that I could do what I like inside it, on the strict understanding that I leave the outside alone other than basic maintenance. Also that I sell back to him when I want to get rid of it.'

'Will you do that some time?'

'At the moment it's unlikely. I've only just got the place in shape.' Jonas shrugged and took her hand in his. 'But I suppose I'll have to part with it eventually. It's no place for children.'

Avery looked up at him sharply, and he laughed.

'No, I don't have any little Mercers right now, but I want a family some time.'

She shivered as the setting sun dipped behind a cloud bank. 'Right now I want that tea you mentioned. By the way, I forgot to ask about dinner. Do I cook it?'

Jonas shook his head, smiling triumphantly. 'I did some shopping on the way. When I told my mother I was bringing a friend she reminded me that I couldn't pick up a phone to order dinner out here in the wilds.'

'Did she know the friend was a female?' enquired Avery.

'She didn't ask, but I told her anyway. Other than pointed regular hints about grandchildren, she's remarkably restrained about the women in my life—probably because I never take anyone home for her to inspect.'

'Have there been many?' Avery couldn't help asking.

'It depends on how you quantify "many",' he said, shrugging. 'The actual number is irrelevant, anyway, because my emotions were never involved. Were yours?'

'To a certain extent, yes,' she admitted reluctantly.

'Morrell?'

She nodded. 'And before him, when I first worked in the City, there was a man called Richard Manners. But that was short-lived,' she added as Jonas went indoors ahead of her to switch on lamps.

'You look cold, darling,' he said as he took her jacket. 'Sit in front of the fire and I'll bring you some tea.'

Avery smiled her thanks and kicked off her shoes to curl up on one of the sofas, wishing Jonas hadn't mentioned his love life, or asked questions about hers. Not that she would let it spoil this time with him, she thought fiercely.

'That's a pensive look,' he commented as he nudged the winged lion aside to make room for the tray.

Avery swung her feet to the floor. 'You were quick.'

'Making tea is not much of a tax on my capabilities,' he assured her, and offered a plate of biscuits.

'I'll just stick to tea,' she said, smiling. 'I ate too much lunch.'

'Or was it my probing about past loves that killed your appetite?' said Jonas, and handed her a tall mug of tea. 'No sugar and a dash of milk.'

'Perfect. Thank you.'

'So, tell me about this Richard Manners,' he said, sitting beside her.

Avery scowled. 'Do I have to?'

'No.' He gave her a penetrating look. 'But if he was a man worthy of your emotions, Avery, I'm curious about him.'

She drank some of her tea before answering. 'I'd had boyfriends in college, of course, but I met Richard soon after I started work, and fell for him like a ton of bricks. He was a lot older than me, but good-looking, very clever, and great fun. He constantly told me he adored me, and because I was young and gullible I believed him. For an entire month I was in heaven. Then the wife he'd forgotten to mention came home from visiting her parents in New Zealand, so that was that. End of story. I had no use for a husband of my own, let alone someone else's.'

Jonas picked up her hand and kissed it. 'And then you met Morrell?'

'Much later. After Richard I steered clear of twosomes. I was much happier as part of a group of people who socialised together on a regular basis. But that finished when I met Paul. He refused to share me with anyone.'

'Is that why you broke up?'

Avery turned quizzical eyes on his intent face. 'You ask a lot of questions.'

'How else will I get answers?'

'Paul and I split up when I resigned my job to look after my mother. I insisted on a clean break.'

Jonas frowned. 'Even though you were in love with him?'

She looked away. 'My feelings had altered by that stage.'

He leaned back, stretching out his legs. 'Is Morrell your reason for the no men rule since you left the City?'

Avery shrugged. 'For the first year at home I was too busy to think about them. And after my mother died I dealt with grief by working all hours to make a success of the business. I had no interest in men, so the local variety soon lost interest in me.'

Jonas moved closer. 'I was luckier than I knew when you accepted my invitation to dinner that night. Why did you?'

'I liked you enough to bend my rules,' she said simply, and looked him in the eye. 'I still do.'

He kissed her hard by way of appreciation, then with a sigh drew away. 'If I start making love to you again right now you'll think that's my sole reason for getting you here.'

'I know perfectly well it's not,' she said, grinning. 'You want me to cook dinner.'

By tacit agreement there was no further mention of the

past. They ate a picnic meal in the main room while they watched mindless Saturday evening television, and an hour or so later he held out his hand.

'Let's do the rest of our viewing in bed.'

Avery followed him upstairs, wondering about the correct attire for watching television in bed. With Paul, bed had been just a place to sleep and make love. He was a restless soul who considered a night at home a waste of valuable time that could have been spent dining out, or in a theatre or some smart nightclub. They had gone to bed late but risen early, as their jobs had demanded, and, looking back on their relationship, one of several things which remained vivid for Avery was a constant feeling of fatigue.

Jonas switched on the television, and then solved her problem by drawing her down on the covers to lean with him against the pillows he'd stacked against the headboard.

'Let's be thoroughly lazy.'

Avery obeyed with a sigh of pleasure as Jonas aimed the remote control and found a televised concert which, since he was more disposed to talk than watch, was the ideal programme for the occasion.

'What do you do when you come here alone?' she asked at one stage.

'As little as possible. But I don't make it here very often. And never,' he added, 'with anyone for company before— unless you count an inspection visit from my parents and my landlord.'

Avery was fiercely pleased. She'd been wondering if another woman had lain here like this with Jonas, and was utterly taken aback by the violence of her objection to the idea. Jealousy was something new in her life. She shivered, and Jonas drew her closer and turned her face up to his.

'Let's go to bed,' he said, in the tone that melted her bones.

Moments later they were under the covers, naked in each

other's arms, all further pretence at watching television abandoned.

'Just lie there,' he whispered, 'and let me make love to every delectable inch of you.'

For a while Avery did her best to comply, but soon found it impossible to lie passive as his hands and mouth travelled over her, causing turbulence wherever they lingered. At last she became impatient, desperate to feel his weight on her body. She dug imperious fingers into his back and Jonas slid up to cover her, holding her hands wide.

'A perfect fit. Even better now,' he whispered, and slid home inside her.

They showered together, ate a midnight feast together, and made love again before they finally went to sleep.

It was very late next morning when Avery woke to the caress of seducing hands, and it was later still when they got downstairs. Jonas drove to the village while Avery grilled bacon and scrambled eggs for a late breakfast. They fell on it like wolves when he came back with the Sunday papers.

'It must be the country air,' she said, putting more bread in the toaster.

'Not entirely,' he said, grinning as she wrinkled her nose at him. 'When can we do this again, darling? I mean the weekend, not the activity that's making you eat like a horse. A very beautiful racehorse, with a gloriously sexy mane,' he added, and touched a hand to her hair.

'As compliments go, that's certainly inventive,' she commented, and put a slice of toast on his plate. 'But the weekend is not always easy for me, Jonas. I can't ask Frances to give up another Saturday for a while, especially now she's seeing so much of Philip.' She sat down and began buttering her own toast, then looked up to meet the eyes which could look so deceptively lazy.

'So what do you suggest, Avery?'

'I suggest,' she repeated deliberately, 'that we enjoy our day together and leave future plans for the future.'

'I would enjoy the day a hell of a sight more if I knew it was to be repeated some day soon. Do you object to night driving?' he asked abruptly.

'No, of course not.'

'Then the solution is simple. You drive here after you close your shop.' Jonas reached to take her hand. 'You could be here in time for dinner.'

Avery was well aware of that, but her pride had demanded the suggestion came from Jonas. 'I could,' she conceded. 'But it might be late before I get here.'

'If you were tired we could always go straight to bed,' he said promptly, and grinned. 'Don't worry—I'd let you have dinner first.'

'If I come—'

'When you come!'

'All right, *when* I come I'll bring dinner with me.'

'And we'll have Sunday lunch in one of the local pubs.' He pressed her hand to his lips. 'But not today. I want you all to myself.'

Avery's eyes dropped, in case his bright, penetrating gaze saw too much. 'It's too late to go out for lunch anyway,' she muttered, ungracious in her need to hide her response.

Outside it was a wet, miserable day that made walking out of the question. But inside the day was perfect to Avery, and they sat together on the sofa that faced the fire and took turns with the various sections of the Sunday paper strewn around them.

Jonas smiled as he showed Avery a shot of a famous model with her equally photogenic toddler. 'Cute little moppet,' he commented.

'Cute mummy, too.' She returned to the book reviews.

'Children not your thing, Avery?' he asked.

'I'm not the maternal type.'

'You don't want children of your own, then?'

Avery shot him a sidelong glance. 'As I've said before, Mr Mercer, you ask a lot of questions.'

He looked at her for a moment, then dropped a kiss on her nose and returned to his paper.

For the rest of the day they lazed about doing nothing at all other than make a meal from the remains of the hamper and tackle the weekend crossword—an activity Jonas found so tiring he took Avery off to bed.

'I thought—you wanted—a rest,' she panted as he kissed the parts of her he was laying bare.

'I want you,' was the terse response. 'Do you want me?'

'Yes,' she said, equally terse, and abandoned herself to Jonas Mercer's idea of an afternoon nap.

Monday had never been Avery's favourite day, and after the idyll of her weekend with Jonas she would have given much to crawl into bed and catch up on her sleep when she arrived back in Gresham Road.

Instead it was a plunge straight into the working week. The run-up to the festive season meant a demand for new partywear, or alterations and repairs to last year's, and Avery was glad of it—and not just from a financial point of view. Plenty of work meant less time for bemoaning the long wait before she saw Jonas again.

The following Saturday he would be involved in a function which required his presence as deputy head of Mercom, and the weekend after that Avery had to put in an appearance at a charity dance for the children's wing at the local hospital.

'A relationship with you, Miss Crawford, is damned hard work,' he'd told her bitterly.

'Likewise, Mr Mercer,' she'd retorted, her voice tart to hide her disappointment.

Knowing that the best part of three weeks would elapse

before they met again, Jonas had kissed Avery goodbye in the dawn of Monday morning with a hunger that in other circumstances would have taken them straight upstairs to bed again. Instead he'd carried her bag to her car, kissed her again at length, and watched her out of sight before he got into his own car to drive to London.

Avery found it difficult to fit back into the comfortable groove that had been her life before Jonas Mercer appeared on the scene. She attended Chamber of Trade meetings, went to concerts and attended plays put on in the small theatre by the local repertory company, but the real highlights of her week were the phone calls from Jonas.

The only person aware of this was Frances—who, as promised, kept the information strictly to herself.

'But to anyone with half an eye to see there's a glow about you these days, Avery,' she said, as they finished for the day. 'I told the others you were on a new course of vitamins.'

Avery laughed. 'Tell me about it! Louise asked what they were and where she could buy them. Luckily I'd noticed that the supermarket had a new line of multivitamins on offer this week.'

'Would it be so terrible, Avery, if people knew you were seeing Jonas Mercer?' asked Frances gently. 'You've had love affairs before.'

'But in anonymous London, not here.'

The location of her affairs had made no difference to her misery when they had ended, but because Avery had kept her social life private from the men she'd worked with in the City it had remained private. Here in the town where she was born it would be different. The interest would be intense if word got out that Avery Crawford was involved with someone as high-profile as Jonas Mercer; even more so when the affair ended. As it would, sooner or later.

*   *   *

In a surprisingly short time Stow Street was ready for reoc-
cupation and Avery signed her new lease. She gratefully
accepted all offers of help, and reported on the move afterwards to Jonas that night when he rang.

'Philip Lester is an organiser, and with the help of Tom
Bennett and Andy Collins, plus the latter's transit van, the
move was made at top speed. Thanks to my wonderful landlord, Avery Alterations is back in town,' she finished with
satisfaction.

'A pity you can't thank your landlord in the way he likes
best,' said Jonas, with a note in his voice which weakened
her knees.

'A great pity,' she agreed huskily.

'It's a hell of a long time until our next weekend together,
Avery. By the way, I've sent you a key. You can let yourself
in if you arrive before me.'

'Thank you—I can make a start on dinner.'

'I don't care a damn about dinner. I just want you there.
In the meantime,' he added, 'be careful at this dance you
insist on going to.'

'I'm not insisting. It's just something I do. My being
treasurer does a lot of good work for the charity—and does
no harm to Avery Alterations, either.'

Jonas laughed. 'You get Frances to do your Saturday and
I'd be happy to give your charity a big fat cheque.'

The annual ball in aid of the children's wing at the local
hospital was a big event held at the Guildhall, beginning
with supper beforehand, and ending with dancing later. As
treasurer to the committee Avery had invited Frances,
Louise and Helen and their men to make up a party at her
table.

'Don't worry,' she had told her team. 'I shall be perfectly
happy to look on as the rest of you trip the light fantastic.'

This was the simple truth. If she couldn't have Jonas for her partner Avery preferred to sit out alone.

In honour of the event all four of them had worked overtime beforehand, to produce evening gowns which would demonstrate the skills of Avery Alterations.

'Nothing like a bit of self-advertisement,' said Frances, twitching jade-green silk into place as they surveyed themselves in the cloakroom.

'The boss outshines us all,' said Louise without rancour. 'With her figure she can wear anything. Though I think you should have left your hair loose, Avery.'

She shook her head. 'A bit over the top with this dress.'

Helen eyed Avery's sleeveless satin sheath with naked envy. 'I just love that shade of crimson, but I stuck to safe old black to minimise the bulges.'

All the tickets had been sold, and the tables surrounding the dance floor were filling rapidly when they joined their men at the table Avery had reserved farthest from the band. Philip Lester got on well with Tom and Andy, despite a decade's difference in age, and, witnessing his undisguised devotion to Frances, Avery felt a glow of triumph over her part in persuading her friend to meet Philip that first night. It had been an inspired move all round. If she hadn't bullied Frances into turning up there would have been no encounter with Jonas Mercer. At the mere thought of him Avery felt a stab of such longing she gave a start when Frances nudged her.

'Look who's just arrived,' hissed her friend.

Avery's eyebrows rose as she watched George and Daphne Morrell join a table of dignitaries with both their sons in tow. 'It's a show of family solidarity for young Dan after the fire,' she muttered. 'Poor kid! He obviously doesn't want to be here.'

'Neither does Paul,' whispered Frances. 'Your ex is not a happy bunny.'

'Am I missing something?' asked Philip, filling their glasses.

'Old flame of Avery's just turned up.'

'Only one?' he said, smiling.

'Probably a few more wannabes in the crowd,' said Andy Collins, grinning at Avery. 'All the lads fancied her in school, but she was too busy passing exams to notice. Tom and I were a few years ahead, but my kid brother had a huge crush on her.'

'Did he really? I never knew!' Avery smiled at him, touched.

During the meal Avery was seated with her back to the Morrells' table, but Frances kept her informed.

'Paul's eyeing your back view a lot.'

'As well he might in this dress,' muttered Avery, wishing Frances had cut it higher in the back.

The moment the tables were cleared the band abandoned background melodies in favour of dance music, and a slim male figure hurried across the floor to Avery.

'May I have this dance, Miss Crawford?' said Dan Morrell.

Oh, boy, thought Avery, but she gave him a friendly smile as she got to her feet. 'With pleasure, Dan.'

He was a little taller than his older brother, able to face Avery at eye level as he placed a respectful arm round her waist. He was trembling slightly as they circled the floor with careful steps the boy had obviously learned by rote. She could almost hear him counting to the beat as they moved to the music, and to divert him asked about his plans for college. Dan relaxed instantly as he described his ambition to be a Queen's Counsel one day.

'Good for you. I can just see you in a wig and gown,' Avery told him, smiling, and caught a look like a thrown dagger from Paul as they passed the Morrell table.

'There's a lot of hard graft before I get to that stage,' Dan said earnestly, then apologised as he missed a step. 'Sorry. I'm rubbish at this kind of thing.'

'You're doing fine,' she assured him.

He smiled gratefully. 'How's your garden?'

'A lot better after your attentions.'

'I could come round any Sunday to give you a hand,' he said eagerly.

'That's very kind of you, but at this time of year the garden doesn't need much in the way of tidying.'

'I'll come in the spring, then, when the grass starts to grow—' He broke off as the music ended. 'Thank you very much, Miss Crawford.'

'My pleasure,' she assured him, and smiled in dismissal instead of letting him escort her back to the table.

'More wine, Avery?' said Philip, brandishing a bottle.

'Water, please.'

'That caused a bit of a stir,' said Frances. 'Daniel's nearest and dearest are a bit put out.'

Avery put her glass down with a sigh. 'I could hardly refuse to dance with the boy. I hope he doesn't ask me again.'

But it was Paul who came next.

Avery moved round the floor with the man she had once been in love with, amazed that the only emotion she felt in response to his proximity was a burning desire for the music to stop so she could go back to her table.

'What do you think you're playing at?' he growled, with a look in his eyes she knew of old. Paul Morrell was furious.

'Elucidate,' she said curtly.

'Leave Danny alone. Is that clear enough?'

Avery looked down at Paul in astonishment. '*He* asked *me* to dance,' she pointed out.

'You made him work in your garden,' he said through his teeth.

Her chin lifted. 'Surely your parents preferred that to seeing him in court?'

'Is revenge sweet, Avery?' he said, his eyes burning into hers.

He had to look up higher than formerly, she thought with malice. Tonight she was wearing heels. 'Revenge?' she said, smiling politely, glad the floor was so crowded by this time that their angry body language would go unnoticed. 'Your mother offered me money to let Daniel off. I didn't take it, but there *was* a fire which affected my business—remember? And Danny & Co *were* responsible.'

'Mother offered you money?' said Paul incredulously.

Avery's smile was cold as ice. 'It surprised me, too. In the past she was never ready with the cash she owed *my* mother.'

Paul looked sick for a moment, his grasp on her fingers painful. 'I can't do anything about that. But if you'll give me the chance I'll do anything you want to make up for my own transgressions—'

'There's nothing you can do Paul, ever,' she said flatly, glad when a break in the music gave her the chance to thank him, so coldly polite that Paul gave her a black look and headed back to his family.

Tom leaned forward, grinning. 'You'd better keep the next one for me, Avery, in case George Morrell is next up to bat.'

'He'd be lucky!' she said, laughing, and then raised an eyebrow as everyone at the table went suddenly quiet. 'What?' she demanded.

Avery spun round in her seat, her eyes incredulous at the unexpected sight of Henry Mason, the Chairman of the Town Council, bearing down on them in company with Jonas Mercer.

'Good evening, everyone. Let me introduce Jonas Mercer of Mercom,' said Henry Mason, smiling genially. 'We had a meeting earlier, and Mr Mercer offered a donation to your charity, Avery. So I suggested he stay on for the dance and hand it over in person to the treasurer.'

'What a good idea,' said the treasurer faintly. She pulled herself together as she took the cheque Jonas held out, and gave him an incandescent smile. 'Come and join us!'

CHAPTER SEVEN

JONAS MERCER blended so effortlessly into Avery's group that none of them left the table to dance. But at last the orchestra leader announced the final number of the first half of the evening, and the entire party took to the floor.

When Jonas took her in his arms Avery knew perfectly well that they were the focus of most eyes in the room, but she no longer cared. Over the protective bulwark of her partner's shoulder she met Paul Morrell's hostile eyes for a second, and in response to the pressure of a long hand on her back moved closer to Jonas.

'I thought it was time I took matters into my own hands,' he said into her ear. 'Do you mind?'

'Do you care if I do?' She glanced up to meet a look that made her heart leap.

'You know—or you should know by now—that I care very much,' he said—a piece of information which cost Avery her timing. 'Even though you're a rotten dancer,' he added.

'I'm not!' she said indignantly.

'Never mind. Even if you can't dance you look sensational,' he informed her. 'But you should have worn your hair down.'

'I tried it that way, but the dress demanded restraint.'

'It's trying my restraint to the limits,' he said conversationally. 'It looks prim and proper from the front, but the back view is lethal. How soon can we leave?'

Avery stifled a laugh. 'Ages yet. Where are you staying?'

'With you—whether the bedroom's tidy or not,' he said, smiling politely.

When people began to leave at last Paul Morrell made a point of coming to the table to wish Avery goodnight. She made the necessary introductions all round, well aware that both men were eyeing each other with interest. Paul chatted politely for a while, murmured something about giving her a call, and rejoined his family.

Avery's party left soon afterwards. Outside in the car park there was a chorus of goodnights all round as Jonas, smiling blandly, stood back with the others to watch her drive off. She arrived home in a state of anticipation which lasted for ten endless minutes before the doorbell rang. She let Jonas in, and without a word he dumped down an overnight bag, seized her in his arms and kissed her very thoroughly.

'I've wanted to do that for hours,' he growled when he raised his head at last.

'Me too. Come to bed,' she added shamelessly.

'I thought you'd never ask!' To her delight Jonas swept her off her feet and carried her upstairs, pressing kisses all over her face as he went. He laid her on her bed, turned her over, and dropped on his knees to press more kisses from the nape of her neck all the way down her spine.

'I've been fantasising about that all evening,' he said with satisfaction, turning her on her back. 'And I bet I wasn't the only one—including Paul Morrell. Sulky little devil, your ex-lover. But there was something familiar about him. I've seen him before somewhere.' He grinned down at her. 'He seemed very peeved about something. Is it possible he doesn't like me?'

Avery gave a hoot of breathless laughter. 'Very possible. He'd like your description of him even less.' She toed off her satin shoes and removed her earrings, relishing the casual intimacy as she watched Jonas dispense with his jacket and shirt. 'His kid brother was there, too,' she told him.

'The pyromaniac?'

'That's the one. Dan rushed across the room to ask me

for the first dance, which didn't go down well at all with Mummy and Daddy. Or with big brother,' she added. 'Paul danced with me to tell me to leave Danny alone.'

'Morrell danced with you to hold you in his arms,' corrected Jonas, throwing his shirt on a chair. He moved to the bed and stood looking down at her, his face suddenly sober. 'I thought of ringing this afternoon, to say I was coming tonight, but in the end I couldn't resist taking you by surprise.'

'And you delighted me in the process,' she admitted huskily.

'I could tell. When you smiled at me I wanted to kiss you brainless.' He sat on the edge of the bed and traced a finger down her cheek. 'I need to make love to you as much as I need to breathe right now. But say the word and I'll just hold you in my arms all night with no more than a chaste kiss if you prefer.'

'Could you really do that?'

His eyes gleamed. 'I could try.'

'Don't even think of it,' she said with feeling, and stood up, presenting her back view to him. 'There's a hook and eye under the little buckle at the back of my neck. Undo it, please.'

'Yes, ma'am!' he said with alacrity. He released the fastener and sucked in a breath as Avery wriggled the crimson satin down and stepped out of it, wearing stockings and a triangle of black lace.

'Dear God, is that all you had on under that dress?' he said, and snatched her up against him.

'I reinforced the top half because I couldn't wear a bra,' she said breathlessly, and smiled at him. 'And I wasn't expecting company when I took it off.' She wreathed her arms round his neck. 'Did you ever see *Gone with the Wind*?'

He blinked. 'Yes, years ago.'

'You remember the part where Clark Gable carries Vivien

Get FREE BOOKS and a FREE GIFT when you play the...

LAS VEGAS

GAME

Just scratch off the gold box with a coin. Then check below to see the gifts you get!

YES! I have scratched off the gold box. Please send me my **2 FREE BOOKS** and **gift for which I qualify**. I understand that I am under no obligation to purchase any books as explained on the back of this card.

306 HDL EFZZ   **106 HDL EFYQ**

FIRST NAME   LAST NAME

ADDRESS

APT.#   CITY

STATE/PROV.   ZIP/POSTAL CODE   (H-P-08/06)

7	7	7	**Worth TWO FREE BOOKS plus a BONUS Mystery Gift!**
🍒	🍒	🍒	**Worth TWO FREE BOOKS!**
🔔	🔔	♣	**TRY AGAIN!**

www.eHarlequin.com

Offer limited to one per household and not valid to current Harlequin Presents® subscribers. All orders subject to approval.

▶ DETACH AND MAIL CARD TODAY! ▶

Leigh up a huge flight of stairs?' Avery sighed and rubbed her cheek against his. 'At the time I thought that was the most erotic thing I'd ever seen.'

'Dressed—or undressed—like this *you* are the most erotic thing I've ever seen,' Jonas said huskily, and kissed her fiercely. 'So carrying you upstairs was a good move on my part?' he demanded after a while, and growled softly as she ran a fingernail down his spine.

'Do I have to spell it out?' she said crossly.

Jonas shook his head and laid her down on the bed. 'I've dreamed about this all week,' he informed her, as he peeled off her stockings. 'Let your hair loose, darling.'

'You're obsessed with my hair,' she scolded, but shook the curling mass free.

'I'm obsessed with every inch of you—including this.' He bent his head to press his lips to the small scar, then stripped off the rest of their clothes and made love to her with a hunger she responded to with fiery abandon after the long days and nights without him.

Over breakfast next morning, Avery informed Jonas that during the night she'd made two important decisions.

He shot her a look. 'Now, why does that worry me, I wonder? Are you about to inform me that this mustn't happen again?'

'Not exactly,' she said, buttering toast.

'Explain,' he ordered.

'I've decided it's high time I stopped letting the past influence the present. Even if there is curiosity about my social life, so what?' She smiled at him. 'I've rather enjoyed having a secret lover, but if you want our relationship out in the open I'm all for it.'

His eyes gleamed. 'You mean it?'

'Yes.'

Jonas reached for her hand and kissed it. 'Good,' he said, and returned to his breakfast. 'And the other discovery?'

'If you fancy more sleepovers here I'll have to get a bigger bed. You take up a lot of room.'

He grinned. 'I thoroughly enjoyed the proximity.'

'Me too, until I almost fell out of bed.'

'In that case, rather than risk injury to your delectable person, order another bed right away and I'll foot the bill.'

'No, thanks. I'll pay for it myself.'

Jonas gave her an exasperated look. 'Without me a new bed wouldn't be necessary. I insist on paying for it.'

Avery poured coffee, smiling at him serenely. 'Insist all you like, but the answer's still no.'

There was silence for a moment, then Jonas, with open reluctance, conceded defeat. 'All right, Avery Crawford. But don't expect to get your own way with me too often.'

'Or you'll draw yourself up to your full height and scare me rigid?'

His eyes locked with hers. 'Don't think I couldn't do it.'

It was the only hint of an argument in a day all the more wonderful for Avery because Jonas's company was such an unexpected bonus. And, because this was the one day of the week when she cooked herself a conventional meal big enough for leftovers, she was able to serve a dish of chicken and rice they polished off in one sitting, along with every vegetable Avery had in the house, plus a large hunk of the local cheese she bought each week in the market. When they finally sat down to coffee afterwards, in a state of mutual somnolence, Jonas smiled at her with a gleam in his eye which told her exactly what he had in mind.

'I fancy a little nap. Are you willing to risk life and limb by coming to bed with me?'

It was the start of a new phase in their relationship. Determined to consolidate on Avery's decision, Jonas managed to get back to Gresham Road again the following weekend, to take her to dinner at the Walnut Tree.

'To achieve this I worked my socks off every day and had to juggle a few appointments. But it was worth it to show we are now officially a couple,' Jonas said with satisfaction, after two of Avery's acquaintances had come to their table angling for an introduction.

'I think the usual term is just "good friends",' she amended. 'Though I'm surprised there are people I know this far afield.'

'Is that why you wanted to come here?' he demanded.

'No.' She smiled at him across the table. 'I wanted to make up for the last time you booked a meal here. This is the dress I meant to wear that night.'

Jonas eyed it with appreciation. 'Something that plain and perfect probably cost an arm and a leg. Or did you make it yourself?'

She shook her head. 'This is the little black dress that all women own in some form or another. But it dates from the time when I earned big bucks in the City.' Avery's fingers played with a long string of natural pearls as she smiled at him. 'And just for you I left my hair loose.'

'Don't think I hadn't noticed! You're blushing,' he added, eyes gleaming. 'What have I said?'

'It's not what you say. It's the way you look at me.'

'As if I could gobble you up,' he agreed.

Avery heaved in a shaky breath. 'This can't possibly last, can it?'

Jonas sobered. 'What do you mean by "this"?'

She leaned forward, her eyes holding his. 'The sex,' she whispered fiercely.

They were back in Gresham Road before Jonas mentioned it again. 'Is that how you think of it?' he asked.

'How I think of what?'

'Back in the Walnut Tree you referred to what happens between us as sex.'

'How would you refer to it?'

Jonas turned her round to face him. 'Whatever word you use to describe the physical part, it's just that: a *part*. I'm attracted to the entire Avery Crawford package, heart and brain as well as looks, plus that independence of yours. Though I'd appreciate a touch more trust in the mix.'

She shrugged. 'I trust you more than any other man I know.'

'After meeting Paul Morrell I don't consider that much of a compliment,' he said dryly.

Avery drew him down on the sofa beside her. 'If you want a compliment, Jonas, you may like to know that the physical part is totally different with you. In the past there was always some part of me that looked on, like a spectator,' she confided, leaning into his warmth. 'With you I forget the world the moment you touch me.'

Jonas kissed her very thoroughly by way of appreciation, then brought up the subject of Christmas.

Avery sighed. 'I'm not doing Christmas this year. I shall just hibernate until it's over.'

'Would that I could hibernate with you, but like a good and dutiful son I spend the day in the bosom of my family. My mother feeds Christmas dinner to a houseful of relatives I don't see much otherwise.' Jonas turned her face up to his. 'But I can be at the Barn early on Boxing Day. Will you join me there, bright and early?'

'Oh, yes, please,' she said fervently, and pulled his head down to hers to kiss him.

Later, as they went upstairs together, Jonas paused on the landing.

'Harking back to our earlier conversation—'

'About sex?'

'If you must reduce everything to the basic, yes.' He

looked down his nose at her. 'I am trying to be noble, so stop interrupting.'

'So sorry. Do carry on.'

'After all this talk of sex, to prove that it is not vital to my enjoyment of your company I'm perfectly willing to sleep in another room tonight, Avery Crawford—no, not perfectly,' he amended, 'but I'm willing to give it a try.'

'Well, you can forget that,' she said bluntly. 'The new bed was delivered two days ago and I haven't slept in it yet. I wanted to share it with you the first time.'

Helen and Louise were involved in large family gatherings for Christmas, as usual, and Frances, who had spent the day with Avery the year before, had been invited to join Philip's daughter and her family. It was taken for granted among Avery's team that she would be sharing the festivities with Jonas, and she was careful to make no mention of spending Christmas Day alone.

In some ways she wasn't sorry for the breathing space. Added to the extra custom in the hectic run-up to the holiday, all four of them had put in a lot of overtime to decorate the windows of the new premises. Their various skills were displayed in scenes from fairy tales, and the result was so successful Avery Alterations had been awarded a large hamper full of seasonal luxuries which Avery divided among her team, keeping her own share of the spoils for her stay with Jonas at the Barn.

After an extra hour in bed in honour of Christmas Day, Avery woke up to a phone call from Jonas to put her in instant festive mood. Later, with the radio for company, she put a ham in the oven to roast, marinated chicken breasts in a garlicky marinade, and then took time over wrapping presents for Jonas. After the ham was done, she rolled the chicken in breadcrumbs mixed with grated cheese and herbs and put it in the oven to cook while she ate a slice of hot ham with the vegetables she'd roasted along with it.

By the time she'd cleared away it was late afternoon, and she took a cup of coffee into the study. She piled more logs on the fire, curled up with the new novel she'd been keeping for the occasion and then groaned in frustration as the door- bell rang. The only neighbours remotely likely to call in were away for the holidays. She waited in case it was carol singers but when the bell rang again there were no voices raised in song. Avery got up reluctantly, went down the hall to open the front door as far as the safety chain allowed, and found Daniel Morrell outside, holding a tall plant.

'Merry Christmas, Miss Crawford,' he said, smiling. 'I wasn't sure you'd be here, but I didn't like to bring this to your shop. It's my personal apology for the fire.'

'How kind. Merry Christmas to you, Dan,' she said, and, masking her reluctance with a smile, led him to the kitchen in preference to the cosy intimacy of the study.

'It's a camellia,' Dan informed her, handing over the plant. 'I thought you could plant it in that blank spot against the back fence.'

'Thank you very much indeed. It's a beauty.' As Avery stood it on the draining board the boy seated himself at the table unasked, with a familiarity that rang warning bells in her head.

'Are you expecting someone?' he asked, eyeing the array of food.

'Yes,' she said promptly. 'I'd offer you coffee, but my visitor will be here soon. Have you had Christmas dinner yet?'

He shook his head. 'We're having it this evening. My grandparents are staying with us—and Paul's home, of course. Did you have good presents? I've got a new com- puter and a digital camera.'

'Lucky you.' Avery glanced at her watch. 'Look, Dan,

I'm sorry to rush you, but I'm expecting my visitor any minute.' She led him down the hall and opened the front door. 'Thank you for sparing time to come round on Christmas Day.'

'I wanted to come. When the weather's milder I could plant the camellia for you,' he offered eagerly.

Avery shook her head, smiling pleasantly. 'That's very kind of you, but I'll enjoy doing that myself. Thank you again, Dan. Enjoy your evening.'

Without warning Dan planted a hard wet kiss on her mouth, then bolted through the door and down the path.

Heart thumping, Avery locked up, scrubbing at her mouth as she rammed bolts home loud enough for Dan to hear if he was still hanging round. Jonas had been right about teen-age hormones, she thought, shaken. She eyed her phone, longing to ring Jonas, but couldn't bring herself to interrupt his family party.

To her great relief Jonas rang for the third time a few minutes later.

'What's wrong?' he demanded.

'How do you know something's wrong?'

'I just do. What happened after I spoke to you last?'

Avery explained, unable to keep the distaste from her voice when she got to the kiss.

Jonas swore volubly. 'I shall have words with Master Morrell—'

'You most certainly will not! I'll handle it myself.'

'Avery, next time he pops round he'll want more than a kiss. Trust me. I was a sixteen-year-old boy myself once.'

'I won't let him in again,' she assured him. 'I had no choice today because he'd brought me a present.'

'Get an intercom installed. You need control over who you let in your house.'

Avery opened her mouth to protest, but thought better of it. 'Very well,' she said meekly.

'No argument? My God, the little bastard really frightened you, didn't he? First he starts a fire in Stow Street, and now he's getting up close and personal.'

'It was my fault for dreaming up that stupid gardening scheme,' she said bitterly.

'The fault is entirely his,' Jonas said forcibly. 'Make sure the house is secure before you go to bed.'

'I did that the moment Danny Boy bolted.' Avery paused. 'I wanted to ring you right away—'

'Then why the hell didn't you?'

'I couldn't interrupt your family party.'

'In future,' he said, very deliberately, 'ring me any time, day or night, if you want me. You *do* want me?'

Was he kidding? 'Oh, yes,' she sighed. 'I want you.'

'Likewise, my darling.' He was silent for a moment. 'Listen, Avery, I've got a change of plan for tomorrow.'

She stared into her wardrobe mirror in sudden panic. 'What do you have in mind?'

'It's pointless for both of us to drive separately. I'll pick you up on my way. Are you happy with that?'

'Yes,' she breathed, limp with relief. 'Very happy indeed.'

'Good. So what are you doing right now?'

'Packing.'

'And after that?'

'I thought I'd take a tray up to my bedroom and stay there.'

'Good idea. If you need me, call, Avery. Promise?'

'I promise. Now, go back to your family, and I'll see you in the morning.'

It seemed ridiculous to go to bed so early, but after loading a tray with everything she needed Avery made sure the fire was safe, left lights on downstairs to preserve the illusion that she had company, set the burglar alarm and went up to shut herself in her bedroom.

When she was propped up in her new bed, with her radio for company, Avery felt embarrassed by her panic over Dan Morrell. He was just a boy overcome by a sudden impulse because he'd found her alone. But when push came to shove things might have turned ugly if he'd wanted more than a kiss. Avery wrinkled her nose in disgust and went on with her book.

Gresham Road was situated in one of the quietest parts of town. When a visit to the bathroom forced Avery to leave her room later, the stillness that surrounded her felt so absolute it chilled. Peace on earth, she reminded herself. She refilled her kettle and went back to her room, resisting the urge to jam a chair under the doorknob. Stupid! She had never felt nervous here before. She could ring Jonas— No, she most definitely could not. It went against the grain to play the little woman in need of protection, especially from a teenage boy.

But after a couple of hours in bed Avery was heartily sick of the arrangement. She got out, turned back the covers, plumped the pillows and went to the bathroom for a shower. But to her intense irritation Hitchcock's *Psycho* popped into her mind as she stood under the spray. She turned off the water hurriedly and rubbed herself dry at top speed, instead of huddling into a towelling robe as usual. She slapped on some of the luxurious bath products Louise and Helen had given her, wrapped herself in her dressing gown, and with a sudden radiant smile rushed across the landing as she heard the phone ring on her bedside table.

'Hello?' she said breathlessly, rubbing at her hair.

'Where were you?' said Jonas.

'In the shower. I got tired of lolling about in bed.'

'Bored with your own company?'

'I certainly am. Is the party over? Where are you?'

'Right outside your front door.'

Avery let out a screech of incredulous delight and hurtled

downstairs. Cursing the burglar alarm for holding her up, she pressed buttons to silence it and unlocked the front door, clumsy with the bolts in her hurry to throw herself into Jonas's outstretched arms.

He lifted her off her feet and walked her backwards as he pushed the door shut behind him, grinning down into her flushed, delighted face. 'Happy Christmas.'

Avery beamed at him. 'It is now! What are you doing here?'

'That business with young Morrell made me uneasy, so God knows what it did to you.' Jonas kissed her swiftly. 'I left the party early, called at the house to collect my gear, and drove here tonight instead of in the morning.'

'Thank you,' said Avery simply, and took him by the hand. 'Are you hungry?'

He shook his head. 'I've eaten far too much today. But whisky wouldn't go amiss. I kept off the alcohol during the festivities because of the drive back to my place—which was an excellent thing in the circumstances.'

'The fire's probably out in the study—'

'I'll see to it while you get the drink,' said Jonas, and pulled her to him suddenly. 'I've got four whole days before I'm due back. How about you?'

'Ditto,' she said triumphantly. 'We're closed until Friday.'

At ten-thirty on the twenty-fifth December that year Avery's Christmas finally began. Curled up on the sofa with Jonas's arm round her, in front of the fire he soon had blazing, it was the perfect end to a day she'd expected to spend alone.

'What did you do last year?' he asked lazily, rubbing his cheek against her hair.

'I spent the day with Frances and her parents. But this year she's with Philip and his family. I hope that works out for her.'

'You did your best to help the romance along,' he reminded her.

'And got my reward, since I met you in the process,' she said with satisfaction.

'What greater reward could you ask?' he said soulfully, but frowned when she got to her feet. 'Where are you going?'

'To get you another drink. You deserve one.'

'Thank you, darling. I like being waited on by a beautiful handmaiden.'

'Don't get too used to it. This is a special occasion,' she said firmly, settling back beside him. 'Very special,' she added. 'Why didn't you ring me to tell me you were coming?'

'You know my passion for surprises. I did think of climbing up to your bedroom window,' he added, with a yawn. 'But I wasn't sure I'd be up for it by the time I got here. And after the incident with Danny Boy it might not have met with your approval.'

'It would have scared the living daylights out of me!'

'A thought which decided me against it.' Jonas dropped a kiss on her hair and settled lower. 'Your welcome was worth every minute on that motorway.'

'You know about my day, so tell me about yours.'

Jonas obliged with a humorous account of greetings from elderly relatives who'd sworn he'd grown taller since their last meeting, of presents that were exclaimed over and endless kissing in acknowledgement, and of his expertise in taking over his father's task of carving the mammoth turkey. But when yawns overtook his narrative Avery stood up.

'Time for bed. Otherwise I might have to carry you there.'

Jonas smiled ruefully as he heaved himself to his feet. 'And, efficient lady though you are, I don't think you could manage that.'

'I know darned well I couldn't! You go on up. I'll just put the fire right, set the alarm and I'll join you.'

He took her in his arms and kissed her with a tenderness which brought a lump to her throat. 'Happy Christmas, Avery.'

'Happy Christmas, Jonas.' She gave him a little push to hide her emotion. 'Off you go. I'll be up in a minute.'

When Avery finally joined him Jonas was stretched out on her new bed, half undressed and fast asleep. She smiled tenderly, pulled the covers over him, then switched out the light and slid in beside him. He muttered something in his sleep and moved closer, and she nestled against him in the warm darkness, utterly happy. Just to have Jonas here beside her was the best Christmas present she'd ever had.

Jonas woke next morning to find Avery asleep beside him, and kissed her awake with such pleasure at the discovery that they were very late for breakfast.

'I apologise for last night,' he said later, as they packed the car. 'My idea was to surprise my lady fair, then carry her off to bed for more X-rated pursuits than sleep.'

She grinned as she tucked an errant curl under the red knitted cap crammed low on her forehead. 'No need for apologies. I was happy with the entire arrangement. Night and morning,' she added, and gave a little shiver. 'I wouldn't have slept so well on my own. The neighbours are away on both sides—a fact which struck home to me when Danny came calling yesterday.'

'I would have been with you earlier last night if I'd known,' he said forcibly. 'I wish you'd let me sort the boy out for you.'

'Absolutely not. I live here. You don't.' Avery smiled at him coaxingly. 'Let's forget Danny and concentrate on each other.'

The four days that followed were the happiest of Avery's

life. Living with Jonas was an addictive pleasure. He was a passionate and demanding lover, but he was also the best companion she could have wished for. He showered her with Christmas presents, some of them inexpensive and humorous, but among them Avery found a pair of earrings hung with large natural pearls to match her necklace, and the largest parcel contained a combination television and video recorder for her bedroom.

'In case you want to barricade yourself in again,' said Jonas, after she'd kissed him.

'Hopefully Danny won't try anything like that again,' said Avery, threading the pearl drops through her earlobes.

'If he does I shall sort him out whatever you say,' said Jonas, then forgot about Daniel Morrell as he unwrapped a box containing a dozen linen handkerchiefs.

'Maybe you don't use the things,' she said, pulling a face, 'but I personalised these.'

Jonas took a closer look and found his initial embroidered in white in different script on each handkerchief. 'You actually found time to embroider all these yourself?' he said incredulously.

'Consider it a labour of love,' she said, smiling. 'Open the other parcel.'

With care he removed the wrappings from a nineteenth-century watercolour, and shot her a look which brought colour to her face. 'Like the donor, Avery, this is exquisite.'

'It's a view of the castle ruins, circa 1840.' She smiled at him. 'It won't go here, with your Greek stuff, but in your office, maybe?'

'I'll hang it in my bedroom in Chiswick.' Jonas moved nearer to kiss her. 'Thank you, darling. Come down to London next time and help me find the right spot for it. It's time you saw my house.'

'I'd just love to, but I can't for a while. Helen and Louise are taking time off until school starts, and I can't expect

Frances to run the show single-handed.' Avery smiled brightly. 'But let's not think of that. As somebody once said to me, let's enjoy the here and now.'

After only a few minutes apart during their entire stay it was a wrench for Avery to leave the Barn on Thursday evening. She had pleaded to stay the night and travel back first thing in the morning, but Jonas was adamant about making sure the security and central heating systems were functioning in Gresham Road before he went back to London.

'I can then leave happy that you're safe and sound. Just remember to keep randy schoolboys away from your door in future,' he ordered.

'Yes, *sir*,' she said, saluting, and took a long last look at the Barn as she got in the car. 'It's so lovely here. I adore this place.'

He smiled indulgently as he drove off. 'We're not leaving it forever.'

She sighed. 'We won't be back for a while, though.'

'True. The first Saturday you can make it I want you with me in London. But be warned—my house is pretty humdrum compared with the Barn.'

'Most places are!'

When they got back to Gresham Street the house felt cold. Avery hurried to switch up the heating she'd left turned low, and Jonas set up the new television in her bedroom, then lit the fire in the study so they could eat their supper in front of it. After the meal Jonas pulled her close.

'Now we're sitting comfortably, this is the point where I make a little speech.'

Avery stiffened. 'About what?'

'In the New Year my father intends to inform the Mercom board of directors that he's handing the reins over to me. He gave me the glad news in the garden on Christmas Day, while he was smoking one of the cigars I gave him.' Jonas stared into the fire, his hand tightening on hers.

'Are you happy at the prospect?' she asked carefully.

'Resigned, rather than happy. Dad's been making noises about playing more golf, travelling more with Mother and so on, but he's not even sixty yet, so I hadn't expected him to retire quite so soon.'

'Is it his health?'

Jonas shook his head. 'I asked him that, but he said this is his way of making sure he stays healthy. He feels he's carried the Mercom baton long enough, so he's handing it on to me.'

Avery looked up at him with misgiving. 'Will this mean a lot of changes in your life?'

'Not that many. I get a bigger office, more responsibility, and a lot more calls on my time, but in the main I'll be doing more or less the same thing I've done for quite a while now. The only change will be the lack of my father's guiding hand. Though even that will be there, ready and waiting, any time I need it. But I'll make sure I don't.'

'Why?'

'If I'm to be head man, Avery, I must damn well behave like it—with no running to Dad for help every time there's a crisis. From tomorrow I'm on my own, without a safety net. I didn't tell you sooner because I was determined nothing would spoil our first Christmas together.'

Avery looked up into the brooding face beneath the thick, glossy hair, and traced a finger over the curves of his mouth. 'You won't have much time for driving up here to see me in future.'

Jonas bit gently on her fingertip, then drew her onto his lap. 'I've thought of a way round that, which brings me to part two of my speech.' He smiled as he felt her tense against him. 'Don't worry. It's a very short speech. We could solve the problem very simply by getting married. I love you, Avery Crawford. Will you marry me?'

CHAPTER EIGHT

AVERY stared at him in such stricken silence that Jonas put her back in her corner of the sofa.

'Not quite the response I expected,' he said wryly. 'I've obviously given you a shock. Shall I get you a drink?'

She shook her head. 'No, thank you.'

He gave her a baffled look. 'Avery, if I hadn't been certain you loved me I wouldn't have said a word.'

'I know,' said Avery miserably. She drew in a deep, shaky breath. 'I do love you, Jonas. So much I can't marry you.'

'What the hell are you talking about? If you love me why can't you marry me? I need to know.' His eyes clashed with hers. 'Is there a husband you've forgotten to tell me about?'

'Of course not.'

'Then what is it?' His mouth twisted. 'I can't believe you carry some melodramatic taint you refuse to pass on to future generations!'

'It's no joking matter,' she said fiercely.

'Do you see me laughing?' he cut back at her. 'After proposing for the first time in my life I think I'm entitled to know why you can't—or won't—say yes.'

'Of course you are.' Avery thrust a hand through her hair in anguish. 'It's my fault. I shouldn't have let things get this far. I knew that from the very first day I came to the Barn.'

He stared at her blankly. 'I thought you loved the place.'

'I do.' Her eyes met his. 'But, as you told me, it's no place for the children you want some day. I can't give you any. So if you marry anyone, Jonas, it should be someone who can.'

'Will you stop talking like some gothic novel and explain?' he said roughly, and seized her hand.

She looked down at the long fingers bruising hers. 'The first time you made love to me I let you assume that I take the necessary Pill. But a few years ago I had an emergency operation which ended my hopes of a family. If you remember,' she added wearily, 'I wasn't keen to let you see my scar. Not because it's so terrible to look at, but for what it represents. But at the time I didn't know—didn't realise—'

'Realise what?' he demanded.

'How it would be between us.' Avery looked up at him in desperation. 'I love you so much it hurts, Jonas. But it wouldn't be fair to marry you. Couldn't we just go on as we are until...?' She trailed away, silenced by the look in his eyes.

'Until such time as I exchange you for a bride capable of providing me with issue?' he said scathingly, and raked a hand through his hair. 'I can't believe this, Avery. I wish to God I'd never mentioned children. I've never thought of them as anything other than a vague possibility in the future some time.'

'But face it, Jonas, there'll come a time when you do want them. And your mother would like some grandchildren right now. You told me that yourself,' she reminded him.

'My mother doesn't come into it.' Jonas seized her by the shoulders, his eyes boring down into hers. 'Are you honestly saying you refuse to marry me over something like this?'

'You make it sound like some trifling kind of whim, but it's *not*!' she said miserably. 'I'm trying hard to do the right thing here, Jonas. After the perfect time we've just spent together do you think this is easy for me?'

His eyes softened and his hands released their grip. 'Of course I don't.' He moved back to his corner of the sofa and sat with legs outstretched, staring into the dying fire. 'Surely there must be other ways round this? IVF, or even adoption?'

'IVF isn't possible for me.' She eyed his profile miserably. 'And even if you were prepared to adopt, and something tells me you're not, I won't marry you knowing that some day you could regret it, Jonas. I'll be your lover for as long as you want me, but—'

'I want you on a permanent basis, as my wife!'

'People don't get married so much these days,' she pointed out.

'I know. I was one of those people until I met you.' He shot a brooding, hostile look at her. 'But now I've met you, Avery Crawford, an occasional weekend just isn't enough any more.'

'Once you've taken over from your father it'll be the only thing possible between us.'

Jonas was silent for a while, then he turned to her with a look which made her uneasy. 'All right. If marriage is out the alternative is simple. We just live together, like those other people you mentioned. You move back to London and share my house.'

Avery frowned as she thought this over. 'You mean I just give up my business and my house? And then what? I sit at home waiting for you like a Stepford wife?'

'Of course not! You could let this house, if you couldn't bring yourself to sell it. Maybe Frances would like to take on the business. And someone with your financial experience would soon find something to do in London.'

'Oh, I see.' Her eyes flashed ominously. 'You have it all worked out for me.'

'Not to your liking, obviously,' he snapped. 'I want a wife. Or, failing that, I'm willing to settle for a partner. But you just want a part-time lover. So it's checkmate.' He was silent for a while, then gave her a searching look. 'Is your problem your reason for ruling men out of your life since you left London, Avery?'

'No. My lack of reproductive skills is nothing to do with it. After I came back here to live I lost all interest in men—until I picked you up that night in the Angel bar.'

'For the first time I wish to God you hadn't!' He rubbed a weary hand over his eyes. 'I can't believe we're having this conversation.'

'I thought we'd never have to.'

'Why?'

'I took it for granted that we'd break up eventually.' She shrugged. 'That our affair was too hot not to cool down, as the song says.'

He turned on her, eyes glittering coldly. 'While I was convinced I'd found the love of my life. But for you it was merely a weekend love affair you could walk away from one day, with no marriage lines to hold you back. Just like the others,' he added harshly.

'You make it sound like hundreds. There were only two!' She jumped up, swallowing hard on the rock-like lump in her throat. 'Jonas, I can't do this any more. I'm going to bed. You've offered to sleep in the guest room before, so tonight I'll take you up on it.'

Jonas shook his head as he got to his feet. He drew himself up to his full height and looked down his nose at her, every inch of him as intimidating as he'd once threatened. 'There's no point in prolonging the agony. I'll leave right away.'

'As you wish.' Head high, she went out into the hall, convinced by the pain in her chest that her heart was breaking. 'Goodbye, then. Thank you for the presents.'

Jonas smiled sardonically as he picked up the bag he hadn't got round to taking upstairs. 'Thank you for mine. It's been a truly memorable Christmas.'

'Very,' she agreed gruffly, and opened the front door. 'Drive safely.'

'Avery, for God's sake!' His eyes locked with hers. 'Is that really all you have to say? Does it have to end between us like this?'

She returned the look steadily. 'Of course it doesn't. It's your choice entirely.'

'And you've made yours,' he said, in a tone which tore her to shreds.

She nodded dumbly, physically unable to say anything else without bursting into tears.

Jonas waited for a moment, but when Avery remained silent he turned on his heel and walked out of the house. He paused in the porch as she was about to close the door. 'I almost forgot. Happy New Year.'

The post-Christmas lull allowed Avery to give Helen and Louise time off until school restarted, and she was deeply grateful that she had only Frances to face when she opened up next morning. A night of sobbing her heart out had done serious damage to her eyes, and her extensive repairs failed to deceive Frances's eagle eye.

'Oh, my dear, what's wrong?'

'Jonas and I broke up last night,' Avery said baldly. 'I had a good cry to get it out of my system, and—and—' To her horror the tears started to flow again.

Frances promptly turned the sign back to 'Closed' on the door, and shooed Avery into the tiny staffroom they'd gained since the enlargement of the shop. 'I'll make coffee. You sit there and cry.'

Avery obeyed helplessly for a while, but at last she scrubbed at her eyes, blew her nose and managed a shaky smile. 'I brought my entire supply of camouflage with me today. I had a feeling I might need it.'

'Good move.' Frances handed her a mug of coffee, then

sat down beside her on the small padded bench built along one wall to save space. 'If you like I'll rattle on about my Christmas and not say a word about yours. Or you can tell me what happened, and why, and I'll keep it strictly to myself.'

Avery sipped her coffee in silence for a moment, then turned to Frances with a look of desperation and began to tell her everything—right from the emergency laparotomy that had ended her hopes of ever having a child to the proposal from Jonas. 'He told me when we first met that he wanted children some day, so I had to turn him down. When I wouldn't budge on the marriage part he suggested I give up my house and the business and move in with him in London.'

'That didn't appeal to you either?'

'Actually, it did.' Avery sighed raggedly. 'But, Frances, I just can't take the gamble. If I did I'd have nothing to come back to when the affair was over. As I know from experience it would be one day.'

'Oh, Avery, I'm so sorry,' said Frances, patting her hand.

'Don't be too sympathetic or you'll start me off again!'

'There's always adoption.'

Avery shook her head. 'Not when Jonas is capable of having children of his own. So here I am, back to single blessedness.' She smiled valiantly. 'But that's quite enough about me, Frances. How was your Christmas?'

'I don't know how to tell you this,' began her friend ruefully. 'But you might as well know straight away. I had a proposal over Christmas, too. But I accepted mine.'

Avery jumped up to hug her. 'That's such wonderful news! I'm so happy for you. Aren't you glad, now, I bullied you into keeping that date with Philip?'

'Of course I am.' Frances eyed her apologetically. 'But it also led to your meeting with Jonas. Do you regret that?'

Avery shook her head decisively. 'At the moment it feels

like the end of the world, but I wouldn't change a thing. My four days of Christmas with Jonas were as near perfection as life gets. Which reminds me,' she added, desperate to change the subject, 'I forgot to tell you about my visit from Danny Morrell!'

Feeling tired, drained, and strangely detached in the aftermath of her tears, Avery checked her phone the moment she was home that night. But the only message was from a security firm asking her to ring to set a time for a visit. What visit? she wondered, and went into the kitchen, rummaging in her bag for her phone. She frowned. She must have left the thing at the shop. Hurray for good old land lines.

She rang the security firm on the kitchen phone and learned that they had been contacted by an employee of the Mercom group, instructing them to install an intercom for her at Gresham Road. Instead of telling them she wanted nothing to do with it Avery made an appointment for the following week, but made it clear that the bill was to be sent to her personally, not to Mercom.

'Frances, have you seen my phone anywhere?' Avery asked next morning.

'No, love. Maybe you left it at home.'

'It's not there, or in the car, so it must be here.'

'Right, let's search,' said Frances briskly.

After a while Avery shook her head. 'No sign of it. I'll have to buy another one. Damn. That's one expense I could do without right now.'

Frances shot a look at her as she got to work on the dress she was altering. 'Did you leave it at the Barn?'

'If I did it can stay there!'

'Have you still got a key?'

Avery closed her eyes in frustration. 'Oh, hell, so I have. Thank you for reminding me; I must post it back to Jonas.'

'Before you do, pop over and look for your phone,' said Frances practically.

'He might be there.'

'Is that such a bad idea?'

'Yes. As Jonas said at the time, there's no point in prolonging the agony.' Avery smiled grimly. 'He's right. I'm a great believer in clean breaks.'

Frances pulled a face as she worked. 'When Sean asked for a divorce I thought my world had ended. But it hadn't. Life went on, and with your help I met Philip.' She looked up. 'You might meet someone else one day, too.'

Avery wanted Jonas Mercer, not someone else.

Due to a plea later from Christine Porter, to shorten a dress she'd sold to a customer to wear to a New Year's Eve dance that very evening, both Avery and Frances worked non-stop to finish all the jobs promised for the big night. Avery shut up shop later with a feeling of anticlimax, wondering what on earth she would do for the next two days until she opened up again.

'I hate to think of you alone tonight,' said Frances, as they walked to the car park together.

'I shall be fine, so don't let it spoil your evening with Philip.' Avery smiled reassuringly. 'I picked up an offer on some classic film videos when I popped out to the supermarket.'

'I'll ring you at midnight to wish you Happy New Year— or maybe not,' said Frances hastily at the look on Avery's face. 'I'll say it now instead.' She gave Avery a hug and walked off quickly to her car.

Avery's long, lonely evening was followed by such a restless night that she woke up in militant mood next morning. The day was fine, and there was no point in moping about at home. She would take Frances's advice and drive to the Barn to look for her phone. And instead of posting the key

to Jonas she would leave it behind afterwards, with a note
to explain her visit.

Avery drove as fast as the legal limit allowed for the
entire journey. When she turned down the track towards the
lake at last she felt a sharp pang of disappointment as the
Barn came into view, and realised that she'd hoped in her
heart of hearts to find Jonas here. But there was no car
outside, so he wasn't.

She stopped just beyond the last cattle grid and reversed
the car onto the grass verge in a good getaway position, but
as she walked the short distance to the Barn her enthusiasm
for her quest evaporated. Searching Jonas's home felt more
and more like illegal entry now she was actually here. She
unlocked the door and keyed in the burglar alarm, then stood
still just inside the lofty room, which looked twice as big
now she was alone here for the first time.

Suddenly she stiffened. The heating was on. Jonas must
be out in his car somewhere. She hated the very thought of
being caught in the act, but now she was here she might as
well look for the wretched phone.

Avery tried hard to think where she'd had it last. She
searched first in the kitchen, then went back to the main
room, all the time keeping an ear cocked for the sound of
a car engine. She peered in vain in the alcove cupboards,
looked along shelves and under rugs. In any other man's
home there would be hundreds of nooks and crannies to
search. Here there was simply space.

At last, afraid Jonas would appear at any moment to ask
what the hell she was up to, Avery rushed up the spiral
stairs at breakneck speed. She got down on her hands and
knees to look underneath the bed—which was unmade and
looked as though Jonas had just got out of it—then hurried
to the dressing room. The familiar scent of something he
used after shaving was everywhere, tormenting her, but she
kept doggedly on with her search. With no luck in the bath-

room afterwards Avery gave it up as a lost cause and ran downstairs. Frustrated and breathless, she took out her new diary and wrote swiftly on one of the blank pages at the back.

I've lost my phone. I thought I might have left it here and came to look for it today, but with no luck. I've left the key. My apologies for the intrusion. Avery.

She read the terse little missive, thought about altering it to try for a warmer tone, but in the end left it as it was. Outside, she wrapped the key in the note and posted it through the locked door, then walked away, feeling more miserable than ever. The phone had been a genuine excuse, but her real motive for coming here had been the hope of seeing Jonas.

Avery had almost reached her car when she heard a shout accompanied by loud barking. She spun round guiltily, her heart thumping as she saw Jonas sprinting towards her with a couple of dogs in hot pursuit.

'Avery—wait!' he shouted.

She had no choice. At the sight of him her feet had taken root. 'Hello,' she said warily, unsure whether she was delighted to see him or sorry she hadn't made her getaway five minutes earlier.

Jonas came to a halt beside her, flushed and windblown in a thick sweater and padded jerkin, but as heavy about the eyes as she was, Avery noted. He ordered the frisking retrievers to sit.

'I left a message at your place to wish you Happy New Year earlier,' he told her, breathing hard.

'You did that when you left last week,' Avery reminded him.

Jonas winced. 'This time I meant it. Come back to the house.'

'No, I'd rather not,' she said, backing away.

'Just for a few minutes. Please.'

Avery eyed him, undecided. 'All right,' she said at last. 'Nice dogs.'

'They belong to my landlord, who is probably skiing down some Alp as we speak. I woke with a hangover this morning and felt like some fresh air, so I drove over to Eardismont to take these chaps for a run. How are you with dogs?'

'Fine.'

'Stay,' ordered Jonas, as the dogs became restive, and both animals obeyed instantly, panting joyously as he lavished praise on their golden heads. 'Meet Castor and Pollux—Cass and Poll to their friends.'

Avery held out her hand palm down as she greeted the dogs, then submitted to some introductory sniffing and licking before scratching them behind their pale silky ears. 'There was no car outside, so I had a look in the house for my phone,' she said awkwardly. 'I thought I might have left it here.'

'I found it behind the toaster this morning,' he informed her. 'In my message I asked if I could call in on my way back to hand it over.'

Before the rift he would have just turned up with it, to give her one of the surprises he was so fond of, she thought sadly.

Jonas gave a curt command to the restless dogs. 'Avery, go inside and make tea or coffee, or whatever, while I take these chaps home and collect my car. I'll be fifteen, twenty minutes tops.'

'You'll have to give me your key, then. I left mine inside, with a note.'

His face set. 'I see.' He fished in his pocket and handed his key over. 'I won't be long.'

Avery watched Jonas and his handsome escorts out of

sight, then unlocked his door again. She picked up her abandoned key and put it with the note beside the winged lion, thinking with longing of the tea Jonas had offered. But making it herself smacked of a familiarity she no longer felt entitled to in the circumstances.

It seemed like a long time before she heard the familiar car. There was a slam of the car door, and then a pause while Jonas exchanged mud-encrusted rubber boots for shoes before entering the room, which immediately shrank to more ordinary proportions.

'I was afraid you wouldn't wait. Sorry I was so long,' he informed her. 'Charlie's housekeeper wanted to give me tea and cakes, and it took a while to extricate myself.'

'It seemed rude to leave before you got back,' Avery said quietly.

Jonas glanced down at the table and picked up the note. He read it, and looked at her quizzically. 'Very terse. Did you make some tea while you were waiting?'

'No.'

'Would you like some now?'

'Yes. Please.'

'Come into the kitchen while I make it, then.'

Almost as though he was afraid she'd take off if he left her alone, thought Avery as Jonas pulled out a chair for her to sit down at the table. He filled the kettle, and said nothing more until he was sitting opposite her with two steaming mugs between them. 'When I returned the phone to you I intended to tell you a story—a true story about my landlord.'

Avery smiled faintly. 'Sounds intriguing.'

Jonas drank some of his tea. 'It's a bittersweet little tale. The main protagonists are close friends of mine. Charlie and I met the first day we started school—'

'Wait a minute,' said Avery. 'Would this be the Charlie who stole your girl?'

'That's the one.'

'And he's your landlord?'

Jonas nodded. 'Tremaynes have been at Eardismont for centuries. So, to revert to my story, Charlie and I were left alone together that first day at school, trying hard not to cry when our parents left. I was tall for my age, but Charlie was small and he was bullied at first. I soon put a stop to that.'

'I can't imagine anyone bullying you,' said Avery.

'Size matters,' he said, shrugging, and went on.

'Years later Charlie Tremayne had been in the sick bay at the time of the first dance at the local girls' school, and had felt hotly envious when Jonas came back with tales of some of the luscious totty on display—in particular one Miss Henrietta Farrar. Jonas had raved about her to all and sundry, so smitten with the lovely Hetty that his peers had egged him on to do something about it.

'So I sneaked out after lights out one night and cycled to the girls' school. I'd lost all enthusiasm for the stunt by the time I got there, but pride made me carry on.' He smiled wryly. 'I could have been expelled, but it was just before exams—not to mention a vital cricket match with a rival school—so in the end I was merely gated. Charlie was fit and well for the end of term party. Miss Farrar took one look at him and I was history. My height and my prowess on the cricket pitch were no match for whatever it is she sees in Charlie.'

'Sees?' said Avery, fascinated.

'They were married the day after he got his degree in Land Management. I was best man.' Jonas tugged his wallet from his back pocket and took out a photograph of a radiantly beautiful girl in bridal white smiling at a short, slim young man with laughing eyes in an otherwise unremarkable face.

'Good heavens,' said Avery in awe. 'She's breathtaking.'

'Even more so now she's older.' Jonas looked down at the snap with affection, then tucked it away again. 'The illness Charlie had in school was mumps. He was pretty ill for a while, and although sterility is pretty rare as a result Charlie is one of the unlucky ones. He can't father little Tremaynes to inherit Eardismont.'

'Ah. I see.' Avery eyed him challengingly. 'There's a moral to your tale?'

Jonas nodded. 'For Charlie and Hetty the only important thing is having each other.'

'Were they married before they knew about Charlie's problem?'

'No. But it made no difference to either of them. If you met them you'd know it was the truth. Charlie's perfectly happy to pass Eardismont on to his nephew as long as he's got Hetty.'

'Very admirable. But if your story was intended as an object lesson it's failed. I still won't marry you, Jonas.'

'I'm not asking you to.'

Colour flooded her face and he jumped up in instant contrition.

'I *meant* that I accept your terms. I want you in my life, Avery. It's as simple as that.' He took her by the hands and drew her to her feet.

Her racing pulse kept her colour high as she gazed up into his face. 'You're willing to be my part-time lover?'

'In preference to the alternative, you've left me no choice,' he said, resigned. 'Only there won't be much part-time from now on, Avery. If you want to see me in future you'll have to come to London. I'm only here now because my father insisted I make the most of the New Year break before applying nose to grindstone.'

Avery was silent for a long time as she looked down at their joined hands. At last she raised her eyes to his. 'All right. We'll give it a try and see how it works out. But now I'm going to say something you won't like.'

'You have to leave?' he demanded, but Avery shook her head impatiently.

'No, not yet. But I think that for a while our relationship should be—well, more temperate.'

Jonas raised an eyebrow. 'No sex?'

'I thought it was making love!'

'It is for me.' He released her hands. 'Come in the other room so we can be comfortable while we thrash out these ground rules of yours.'

'They're not rules,' she protested. 'I just want to explain something.'

Avery sat down on one of the sofas, but instead of sitting beside her Jonas took the one opposite.

'Fire away,' he said briskly.

Avery took in a deep breath, hoping her colour would diminish some time soon. 'Until I met you I believed that my operation had killed my libido stone-dead,' she said bluntly. 'But it took only one kiss from you to bring it back to life.' She looked at him in appeal. 'I know that side of a relationship is important—'

'But from now on,' said Jonas, 'you think I shouldn't take you to bed the minute I'm through the door.'

'You're not taking this seriously!'

'I'm deadly serious.' He leaned forward, hands clasped between his knees. 'In future, even if we spend long intervals apart, I promise I won't rush you to bed the minute I lay eyes on you. But being a normal sort of bloke, Avery, I'll want to.'

Wishing she hadn't started this, Avery got up. 'I'd better be going.'

'Why?' said Jonas, jumping up to forestall her. 'Is there something—or someone—waiting for you?'

'No,' she admitted reluctantly.

'Then stay. Please. Let's make the most of this bonus time right now, Avery. Just spending time together—doing the crossword, going for a walk, listening to music—whatever you want.'

She looked at him levelly. 'You mean stay the night?'

'Yes.'

'I didn't bring any clothes.'

'Borrow something of mine.' The compelling, fatigue-smudged eyes held hers with such determined persuasion Avery couldn't have resisted even if she'd wanted to.

She nodded slowly. 'All right. Do you have any food?'

CHAPTER NINE

THE immediate catering problem was solved by lunch in the low-beamed, friendly atmosphere of one of the village pubs. After the meal Jonas, well known from his frequent stays at Eardismont, was asked to play darts, and Avery applauded wildly when he hit a showy bullseye.

Watching him as he laughed with the other dart players, she felt passionately grateful that they were together again. But passion was playing no part in their reconciliation so far. If she'd pictured a reunion at all it would have included making love as the first step. Instead they'd walked to the pub, talked without constraint as they ate, and eased back into their relationship by degrees.

'I enjoyed that,' said Avery, as they walked back through the cold, crisp afternoon. 'I didn't know you were a whiz with the arrows.'

He grinned. 'I'm good, but Charlie's better—and Hetty can whip both of us. How about you?'

'Not bad, but I haven't played since college.'

'Next time I'll take you on at the pub.' As they reached the first cattle grid on Eardismont land Jonas took her hand. 'Were you at a party last night?'

'No. Were you?'

He shook his head. 'I was here. Alone.'

'I pictured you in London at some smart social gathering,' she said casually.

'I could have been.' He looked down at her, his grasp tightening. 'For some reason I wasn't in the mood.'

'I don't like New Year's Eve parties,' Avery confessed.

'To me there's something melancholy about the passing of the old year. I can't take all that meaningless kissing either.'

'I can't say I agree with you there,' said Jonas, grinning. 'Give me your keys. I'll drive your car up to the Barn.'

'I'll make the most of the weather and walk the rest of the way. You can put the kettle on,' she said, as he folded himself into the driving seat.

Jonas looked up at her through the open car window. 'I'll do anything you want. Always.'

Avery was very thoughtful as she walked slowly down the track to the Barn. Always was a long time.

She shrugged off her fey mood, watching curiously as Jonas took a box from his car before going in the house.

'What was in that mysterious package?' she asked when she joined him.

'I was in such a hurry to get back here after I'd returned the dogs I forgot that Mrs Holmes had given me a pie,' he informed her.

'Who is Mrs Holmes?'

'She's Charlie's housekeeper. I've known her since I was thirteen—I used to spend part of every school holiday here. When I went over this morning she was baking a batch of these for the freezer.' Jonas led Avery into the kitchen, where an outsize pie, still giving off a mouth-watering aroma, sat on the table beside an equally large fruitcake.

'What a glorious smell!' she exclaimed. 'No problem about dinner, then.'

'Afternoon tea first,' he informed her. 'The tray's in the other room. I'll bring the cake.'

Two slices of cake and a large quantity of tea had been consumed before there was much conversation.

'The walk made me hungry,' said Avery. And she hadn't eaten much lately, either. Just being with Jonas had kick-started her appetite. She took off her shoes and curled up on the sofa, watching the flames flickering on the pebbles in the wall-mounted fireplace.

'What did you do last night?' asked Jonas, leaning back beside her.

'I watched some videos until the usual fireworks signalled zero hour, at which point I drank a glass of wine in toast to my mother. Even in my partygoing London days I always took some leave at this time of year so I could spend Christmas and New Year's Eve at home with her.'

'This year we should have been together,' said Jonas with sudden bitterness.

'You were the one who walked out.'

'Not without reason.' He stared into the fire. 'Your rejection was a body-blow.'

'I rejected your proposal, Jonas, not you personally. Not that I cared for your rearrangement of my life much,' she admitted bluntly. 'But I suppose it's understandable. You're used to people who jump when you say jump.'

He turned to look at her. 'I didn't mean it that way. I just took it for granted that after what you told me about your childhood you'd be glad to turn your back on your home town.'

'In some ways I would. But if I sold the house and the business I'd have nothing to fall back on in the future when—'

'When I find someone to mother these mythical children of mine,' he finished for her.

'When we're no longer together,' she said, glaring at him.

'That isn't going to happen!' He seized her by the shoulders. 'My name is Mercer, not Morrell. I don't know what the bastard did to destroy your faith in mankind, Avery, but it's time to put it behind you and cultivate some trust where I'm concerned. We're going to stay together, married or not. I love you, Avery. Nothing's going to change that. I swear it.'

Tears hung on her lashes as she gazed up at him. 'But what happens when the time comes for you to hand on the Mercom baton?'

'No problem. I don't have a nephew, like Charlie, but I've got a couple of young cousins only too ready to snatch the baton from me any time I want to hand it over—if not before.' Jonas released her, and then pushed her sweater aside on her shoulder, his eyes remorseful when he saw the marks his fingers had made on her skin. 'I'm sorry, darling.' He laid his lips to the faint bruises and looked up, his eyes darkening as they met hers. 'In the interests of this temperance you wanted,' he whispered, 'I haven't even kissed you yet.'

She raised her face to his in prompt invitation, and Jonas took her in his arms. But instead of crushing his mouth to hers he held her tightly, rubbing his cheek against hers. 'Happy New Year, Avery. And this time I mean it.'

'Happy New Year, Jonas.' She tipped her head back to smile at him. 'I really believe it will be now.'

He kissed her at last with a tenderness which soothed away all the anguish of the past few days. 'Let's make a deal. In future all quarrels, fights and disagreements must be followed by immediate reconciliation.'

'You were the one who walked away.'

'Are you ever going to let me forget that?'

'Probably not. I'll keep reminding you until you're old and grey!'

'Promise to stay with me that long, darling, and you can remind me as much as you like.'

Avery held out her hand. 'In that case, it's a deal.'

Jonas shook her hand solemnly. 'Deal.'

It was a very different day from any spent at the Barn together before. Jonas, Avery soon realised, had taken her plea for temperance to heart. They talked, read the papers, put some music on while they did the crossword, and although he gave her a fleeting kiss in passing now and again, as they put dinner together, they watched television afterwards from one of the sofas in the living room instead of the bed upstairs.

In some ways Avery was glad, in others she felt unexpected pique over Jonas's restraint, and in the end, with a view to bringing matters to a head, asked him if he had a spare toothbrush.

'Ready for bed?' he asked, jumping to his feet.

She nodded matter-of-factly. 'I haven't had much sleep lately.'

'You'd better give me a few minutes to change the sheets.' He grinned ruefully. 'I wasn't expecting company.'

'We'll do it together.'

The ordinary domesticity of stripping the bed and wrestling the duvet into a clean cover eased the tension which had been mounting between them during the evening as bedtime approached. Jonas dumped the used linen in the bathroom hamper, but couldn't find a spare toothbrush on the shelves—something Avery could have told him and spared him the search.

'If you don't mind sharing I'll use yours,' she said briskly.

He gave her a graceful bow. 'I'll be honoured. You can even use it first. Am I a gentleman, or what? What else does madam require?'

Avery ticked off her fingers. 'Your towelling robe, so I can have a shower, and a T-shirt and some boxers, please.'

'Coming right up. Any colour preference?'

'You choose.'

Jonas went into the dressing room and came back with a white T-shirt, navy boxers, and a crimson towelling robe he removed from its polythene bag before handing it to Avery. 'Christmas present from my mother,' he informed her.

'How sumptuous,' she said, smoothing the pile, and reached up to kiss his cheek. 'Thank you.'

Jonas caught her by the elbows to pull her up on her toes, gave her a kiss that left them both breathless, and then tapped her on the seat of her jeans. 'Off you go,' he said gruffly.

In future, decided Avery, as she did some quick hand washing before her shower, she would travel everywhere with a change of underwear and a clean shirt. Glad she'd chosen to wear the fetching navy lace set Frances had given her for Christmas, she rolled her laundry in a towel, draped it on the radiator, and then, careful not to wet her hair, lathered herself in the shower with some of Jonas's gel.

She dried herself roughly and wrapped herself in the crimson robe. Decision time, she thought, eyeing the boxers and T-shirt. She could put them on and look ludicrous, and maybe send out entirely the wrong signal to Jonas, or she could just stick to the robe, which looked a great deal more alluring and hopefully gave out exactly the right signal. No contest, then.

She slapped on some moisturiser from the small bag of cosmetics which, unlike spare underwear, travelled everywhere with her, then brushed hair that had turned riotous from the steam. She went into the other room to find Jonas lying on the bed, watching a late-night newscast. He turned quickly, and gave her a look which stopped her in her tracks.

'Lady in red,' he said huskily. 'That looks a lot better on you than it ever will on me. How about the other things— do they swamp you?'

'I haven't tried them yet. I thought you might want a shower.'

Jonas slid to his feet. 'Which kind do you recommend? Hot or cold?'

Avery smiled slowly. 'Oh, hot. Definitely hot. It's no

weather for cold showers. Don't be long,' she added, to make sure he got the message.

'Five minutes!'

When Jonas reappeared in less than four, with a towel knotted round his lean hips, the crimson robe was on a chair, the television was switched off and Avery lay in bed with the covers up to her chin.

'That was quick,' she said breathlessly.

'What did you expect?' He threw the towel on the floor and slid into bed, pulling her naked body against his. 'I hope you expected *this*,' he said against her mouth, and slid his hands under her bottom to pull her closer. 'A man can't hide his basic needs.'

'Neither can a woman, if a man knows where to look,' she said, and blushed to the roots of her hair at the look he gave her.

'God, I want you so *much*!' He crushed his mouth to hers as his invading fingers showed he knew exactly where to look. He found the little engorged bud waiting for him, caressing it with such tormenting expertise Avery gave a husky little moan which cost Jonas his control. He surged between the long, slender thighs which locked round his hips so fiercely that their mating was savagely short, but so blissfully sweet they lay together afterwards, unwilling to separate in the heady relief of reconciliation.

But at last Jonas turned on his side, smoothing Avery's head against his shoulder, and she relaxed against him with a sigh, her last conscious thought one of thanksgiving that they were together again.

Next morning Jonas woke Avery up with the demand that she stay at the Barn with him until the last possible minute the following morning, and she blinked at him sleepily, nodding in agreement.

'I'll have to take off at crack of dawn, but you don't have to,' he told her.

She shook her head. 'When you go, I go.'

He held her close, rubbing his cheek over her wildly untidy hair. 'I wish you were coming with me to London.'

'I am coming—in a fortnight's time,' she reminded him. 'I'll travel down on the Saturday night—'

'And stay until Monday morning?'

Avery looked up into his intent eyes. 'I'd thought to come back on the Sunday evening, but I suppose an early train the next day is a possibility.'

'It would give us another night together. Make that definite and I'll take you somewhere special for lunch today.'

'I don't have the clothes for ''special'',' she protested.

'You don't need clothes to look special,' he said, in a tone which brought colour to her face. 'In fact,' he said, kissing her hungrily, 'I like you best the way you are right now.'

Avery kissed him back, and, since she was lying naked in his arms at the time, Jonas took the kiss as encouragement, and began to make love to her with all the skill and finesse he'd been incapable of in the desperate frenzy of the night before. Afterwards, shaken by the intensity of the feelings they'd roused in each other, they stared into each other's dazed eyes as their heartbeats slowed.

'I love you, Avery,' said Jonas at last, in a tone she'd never heard before.

'I love you, too, Jonas,' she said unsteadily, and buried her face against his shoulder.

The 'somewhere special' was a small, unpretentious pub deep in the Marches. Jonas had to duck to miss the overhead beams when they left the bar for the small, crowded dining room, where they were shown to a table in the window embrasure.

'This is a very attractive place,' said Avery, looking round with pleasure.

'I came here first with Charlie and Hetty. It's pretty pop-

ular with those in the know. I was lucky to get a table.
You'll see why when you taste the food!'

'I hope I will soon. I'm starving.'

'You should have had some breakfast.'

'It was so late by the time we got up there was no point,'
she said, smiling at him, and saw his eyes darken.

'In certain circumstances,' he said softly, 'I'm happy to
forgo breakfast every time.'

There was no more conversation between them once their
meal arrived, other than sounds of appreciation as they ate
shanks of lamb braised to gluey perfection in red wine and
served on a bed of perfect vegetables.

'That was delectable,' Jonas told the girl who removed
their plates. 'Please pass on the message.' He frowned as
he saw the look on Avery's face. 'What's wrong, darling?'

'I can't believe this.' She turned her head away to look
out of the window. 'Paul Morrell just came in.'

'Do you want to leave right now?' asked Jonas quietly.

'Would you mind? Let's have coffee in front of those
pebbles of yours.'

Since the only way out led past Paul Morrell's table, he
was on his feet by the time they reached it.

'Hello, Paul,' Avery said, resigned.

'Hello, there,' he said, his smile bright but his eyes cold
as they fastened on Jonas. 'Fancy meeting you two here. I
read about this place in the press last week. Obviously you
did, too.'

Jonas shook his head. 'Friends brought me here some
time ago—before it achieved fame.'

'Since Paul's forgotten to introduce me, I'll do it myself,'
said the woman with him. 'Annette Hughes. I work for
Paul's father. Nice to see you, Avery.'

'You too, Annette,' said Avery serenely. 'This is Jonas
Mercer—the man responsible for our new cinema.'

'I read about it in the local rag. Nice work,' said Annette with approval. 'When does construction start?'

'Tomorrow,' Jonas informed her, and looked round as a waitress approached with a laden tray. 'We're in the way. If you'll excuse us, we must get back.'

'To town?' said Paul.

'Not today,' said Avery coolly. 'We're celebrating the New Year break at Jonas's weekend place on the Eardismont estate.' She smiled warmly at Annette and strolled from the room, with Jonas close behind her.

Avery went outside to the car while Jonas paid the bill, glad of the cool air on her face.

'Way to go, Tiger,' said Jonas as he joined her. 'That was fighting talk back there.'

'Do you mind?'

Jonas took her in his arms and kissed her in full view of anyone who might be looking, then opened the car door for her. 'No, my darling, I don't mind at all. But Morrell minds like hell. I suppose you know that he's still hopelessly in love with you?'

'Hopeless is the right word.' Avery settled back in her seat as Jonas drove off. 'I've contacted him only once since we broke up, to ask who'd taken over the lease of my business. That was the day I spat fire at you when you came to take me out to dinner.'

'So it was his fault,' said Jonas grimly.

'To be fair, it was mine,' said Avery. 'I bawled you out before you gave me the facts.' She laid her hand on his knee. 'Sorry, darling.'

He covered her hand with his for a moment. 'You call me darling for the first time when I'm driving, I notice, when I can't show my appreciation.'

'You showed quite a lot of appreciation just now outside the pub,' she reminded him, smiling. 'Do you think Paul was watching?'

'I don't give a damn whether he was watching or not. After hearing that little declaration of yours I just needed to kiss you. In case you're interested, I still do,' he added with a sidelong glance.

'I am. Deeply interested,' she informed him, and stroked his thigh again, delighted when his muscles tautened under his touch.

'If you do that again I won't answer for the consequences,' he said through his teeth.

'Then I'll leave it until we get home.'

'I'll keep you to that!'

For the rest of their time at the Barn they restricted their outings to a trip to the village to buy milk, bread and the daily paper, and made a meal from the supplies Jonas had brought with him.

'I wish I could crystallise every minute and put it aside to look at later when we're apart,' said Avery at one point.

'If you came to live with me in London we wouldn't have to be apart at all, other than during my working day,' he reminded her.

It was a prospect that began to monopolise Avery's thoughts when she had a moment to herself, which was usually in the bathroom. Jonas was reluctant to let her out of his sight otherwise, but Avery made no protest, equally unwilling to be parted from him for a second longer than was necessary.

And that night they made love with a feverish intensity, as though the coming parting added a new dimension to their need for one another.

They were up cruelly early in the morning, and when Jonas was ready to leave, dressed in formal City suit, he turned to Avery.

'How do I look?' he asked.

'Impressive; every inch the Chief Executive,' she assured

him, and cleared her throat. 'I won't come out to the car. I'll say goodbye in here.'

Jonas took her in his arms. 'I'll be there at the station to meet you on Saturday week. Make sure you don't miss the train.'

'I won't.' She held her face up for his kiss. 'Drive safely.'

'I'll ring you tonight,' he promised, and kissed her again. They held each other close for a moment, then Jonas picked up his suit bag and grip and went out to the car.

Jonas turned to see Avery watching at the window and blew her a kiss. She returned the favour, then watched the car until it was lost to sight.

CHAPTER TEN

WHEN Frances arrived at the shop a couple of hours later she took one look at Avery and let out a huge sigh of relief. 'You've made it up.'

Avery nodded happily. 'Jonas was at the Barn. He'd spent New Year's Eve alone and miserable, too. He says he'd rather have childless me than fruitful someone else, so in the end I stopped arguing.'

'Excellent news. When Helen and Louise get back can we stop trying to fob them off with tales of wonder vitamins and confirm the real reason for your glow?'

'Why not? From now on the whole town can know.'

Frances chuckled. 'After Jonas's appearance at the dance no one will be surprised.' She looked up suddenly. 'What's that noise?'

Avery went to the door and looked out, and saw Nadine from the florist at the end of the street. 'What's going on?' she called.

Nadine raised a triumphant thumb. 'The Mercom bulldozers have arrived, Avery. We'll have our cinema soon!'

High hoardings soon enclosed the site, and other than some unavoidable noise there was little effect on the daily commercial life in Stow Street—apart from a big increase in custom for the café, which fed the construction workers from day one. And for Avery it meant a possessive little thrill every time she saw the big Mercom signs on the hoardings on her way to and from the car park.

'I wish I had time to check on progress myself,' said Jonas, when she confided this during one of their late-night telephone conversations.

'Is it tough at the top?' she asked with sympathy.

'Damn right it is. I respect my father more with every passing hour when I realise how much he packed in to a day. But I'll make sure nothing interferes with our weekend together, darling. So don't miss that train!'

When Frances heard Avery intended leaving on a late-afternoon train for her trip to London she insisted on coming in for that afternoon to let Avery leave earlier. Making a vow to buy Frances the best wedding present she could find, Avery accepted the offer gladly, delighted to be able to spring a surprise on Jonas for a change. But before that happy day, she thought with a sigh, there was a weekend in Gresham Road to get through, plus the following interminable week.

Sunday was fine, and so mild for January that Avery decided to kill time by planting the camellia Dan Morrell had given her. In sweatshirt, jogging pants and rubber boots she unlocked the shed, pulled on heavy-duty gloves and loaded tools and half a sack of compost on the wheelbarrow. She pushed it to a vacant spot along the back hedge and began digging. When the hole was big enough she lined it with compost and went back up to the house to fill the watering can, but as she switched off the outside tap a man appeared round the corner of the house. In contrast to her muddy, dishevelled person, her unwanted visitor was a vision straight from the pages of *GQ*.

'Hello, Avery,' said Paul Morrell, biting back a grin at the sight of her. 'Busy?'

'Obviously,' she retorted. 'What do you want?'

'Just a chat. Can I come in?'

'The answer's still no. You never give up, do you?'

He scowled. 'If you won't let me in the house at least talk to me while you carry on with your gardening.'

Avery shrugged, and took the watering can back down the garden.

Paul followed her to the hole, wincing as his shoes squelched in wet grass, and stood with arms folded, watching as Avery took the camellia from its pot. She planted it carefully and watered it in, then mulched it with more compost before giving Paul her attention.

'So why are you here? You're dogging my footsteps a whole lot more than I care for lately.'

He shrugged. 'My presence at that dance was a royal command from the parents. But the encounter at the Ivy Bush last week was pure coincidence. Are things serious between you and Mercer?' he added abruptly.

Avery shot him a cold glance as she loaded the wheelbarrow. 'Why? What business is that of yours?'

'You know damn well I still have feelings for you, Avery. I'd hate to see you get hurt.'

She gave a bark of scornful laughter. 'That's rich, coming from you.'

His eyes glittered angrily. 'I asked around. Apparently Mercer's got quite a track record with women.'

'For a heterosexual male of his age that's normal, surely?'

'Are you in love with him?'

Avery met his eyes squarely. 'Yes, Paul, I am. I also like Jonas enormously and enjoy his company. I even respect him, which is a welcome change in my dealings with men,' she added, very deliberately.

He flinched. 'God, Avery, you know how to put the knife in!'

'I should do—I was taught by masters,' she said sweetly. 'Now, if you don't mind I need to clean up. Oh, and by the way, kindly inform your brother that he's no more welcome here than you are.'

Paul frowned. 'Is Danny in the habit of coming here, then?'

'Certainly not. He's been here just once since the gardening session. He came round on Christmas Day, to give me the camellia I've just planted.'

'So that's where he went! The little devil told Mother he went to see a pal to show off his new camera.' Paul raised an eyebrow. 'Was Mercer with you at the time?'

'No, he arrived later.'

'So you were alone.' His eyes narrowed. 'Did Danny ask for a kiss in return for his present?'

'He took, not asked!'

Paul swore viciously. 'Did he get out of hand?' He pulled the barrow away to seize her by the elbows. 'Tell me!'

Avery shrugged. 'It was no big deal. Just a kiss.'

Paul's eyes glittered with fury. 'I'll make sure the little tyke doesn't try it again.'

She raised a scornful eyebrow. 'That's a change of heart. At the dance you warned me off him.'

'I needed an excuse to dance with you. God knows there's no other way to get you in my arms again,' he said morosely, and shot a pleading look at her. 'Is there?'

Avery detached herself firmly. 'Absolutely none.'

A pulse throbbed at the corner of his mouth. 'But I still love you, Avery. Are you really going to marry Jonas Mercer?'

'Yes, I am,' she lied, wanting to put an end to this once and for all. But with a despairing groan Paul pulled her against him and crushed his mouth to hers. The next moment he was sprawling on the grass with his young brother standing over him, fists clenched.

'Leave her alone!' shouted the boy.

Scarlet with rage, Paul leapt to his feet and lashed into his brother with such fury they overbalanced and fell to the grass in a struggling, grunting heap.

'Will you both stop this?' said Avery, incensed. When neither of the Morrells paid her any attention she ran to fill the watering can, and returned to stand over the combatants.

'Right, then, you asked for it!' she warned, and poured a flood of ice-cold water over their heads.

The pair gasped and spluttered as they scrambled up, pushing wet hair from streaming faces.

'Why the hell did you do that?' howled Paul, brushing frantically at his cashmere sweater.

'I came to your *rescue*!' gasped Dan in reproach.

'What the hell are you doing here, anyway?' demanded Paul angrily.

'I came to help Miss Crawford in the garden and found you mauling her about,' said the boy hotly. 'You make me sick!'

'That's enough,' ordered Avery. 'I'd like you both to leave now, please.'

'Avery—' began Paul, but she made a short chopping motion with her hand.

'Enough,' she repeated flatly, and looked at them both in turn. 'Don't even think of coming anywhere near my house again in future—either of you.'

Dan reacted to her words like a whipped puppy, but Paul gave Avery a look of such menace it raised the hairs on the back of her neck. For a moment his eyes glared murderously into hers, but at last he turned on his heel and strode off, with his brother trailing disconsolately behind him.

Avery put the unpleasant incident behind her, and decided not to mention it to anyone—especially Jonas. And she travelled down to London on the early train the following Saturday in a state of happy anticipation at the thought of taking him by surprise.

Her taxi dropped Avery outside a house in Chiswick that was so much the opposite of the Barn she stared in amazement, finding it hard to believe that the same man owned both of them. The large, conventional house had probably been built at the same time as her own, but this one was in a different league on the property ladder, with huge windows and a third storey. In a fever of anticipation she hurried up the wide drive to the white-painted front door and pressed the bell.

'Surprise, surprise,' she said joyfully when the familiar voice answered through the intercom. 'It's me.'

When the door opened Avery's radiant smile faded as she met the look in Jonas's eyes.

'You're too early,' he said in a tone she'd never heard before. Then she saw the glass in his hand.

'Is something wrong?' she asked as he closed the door behind her.

'Yes, it is,' he said, swaying slightly. 'I'm coming to terms with bereavement.'

Avery dumped her bag down and went to him with swift compassion. 'Oh, darling, I'm sorry. Who—?'

'Not who,' he contradicted. 'What.'

In spite of her shearling jacket Avery suddenly felt cold. 'What do you mean?'

His smile froze Avery's blood. 'I've known quite a lot of women, but not one of them was remotely like you. You're one of a kind, Avery Crawford.'

'That's obviously not a compliment.' She took in a deep, calming breath. 'Tell me about this bereavement.'

'You'd better come in here,' he said, and led the way—unsteadily, she noticed with foreboding—into a big room at the back of the house. 'I refer to the murder of my illusions,' Jonas said with drama, slurring the consonants. '*J'accuse*, Avery Crawford. You're the assassin.'

'And you're drunk.' And dangerous, she thought apprehensively.

He gave a bark of laughter and made a lunge for the tray of bottles on a side table. 'Need 'nother drink,' he muttered.

Avery intercepted him and removed the glass from his hand. 'First tell me what this is all about.'

Jonas drew himself up to his full height to glare down his nose at her, then swayed precariously, spoiling the effect.

'You'd better sit down before you fall down,' she ordered, and took him by the arm to pull him to a leather chesterfield.

Jonas slumped down on it, eyeing her malevolently. 'I drank myself into a stupor last night, and slept late. When I surfaced I rang your shop to tell you to stay away from me, but Frances said you'd already left. So here we are—man to man. Man to woman,' he corrected.

Feeling hot suddenly, Avery removed her sheepskin jacket.

'Sit down,' Jonas ordered. 'It makes my head thump to look up so far.'

Avery sat down on the edge of a studded leather chair a little distance away, and looked at Jonas in despairing silence. In his present mood it seemed pointless to demand explanations. She'd never seen him the worse for drink before and had no idea what to do. But silence was supposed to make people talk to fill the vacuum. Maybe it would work on Jonas.

'Cat got your tongue?' he demanded, after a while.

She shook her head.

'Don't you want to know what's wrong?'

'Of course I do.'

'I met a chum of yours yesterday. Well, not *met*, exactly. I was in El Vino's, having a drink with a friend of mine before that City dinner I mentioned. And who should follow me into the men's room but your buddy, Paul Morrell? That's why he was familiar, y'know. I'd seen him there before—in El Vino's, I mean, not lurking in the gents'.' Jonas struggled to his feet. 'I need that drink.'

'No, you don't.' Avery jumped up and gave him a push, which landed him back on the sofa. 'Talk first. Drink afterwards.'

He glared up at her. 'Don't order me about, woman. I want a bloody *drink*.'

'You can have one after you've told me what Paul did to put you in this state.'

'Said, not did.'

Avery met his eyes steadily. 'What did he say, then, to cause all this melodrama?'

Jonas gave another bark of mirthless laughter. 'Good word. You hit the nail right on the head. Your friend Paul *said* something ve-e-ry interesting. He said you were going to marry me.' He wagged a finger at her. 'I didn't know that. But here comes the interesting part. He advised me to reconsider, because he knows for a fact that you can't have children.'

'You know that already,' she said quietly.

'True. But he told me *why*, Avery. You forgot to mention that you and Paul Morrell had a child together.' His eyes stabbed hers like dull steel blades. 'According to him, it was the birth of this child that made it impossible for you to have any more.'

'That's right,' she said without inflection.

'It's *true*?' He stared at her, his face suddenly so haggard Avery realised he'd been hoping Paul had lied. 'So what happened? Did you have the child adopted?' His mouth twisted in a sneer. 'Stupid question! With your background what else would you do! Morrell wouldn't marry you, I suppose. And Avery Crawford couldn't possibly let history repeat itself—'

He broke off with a grunt as Avery slapped him hard around the face. For a frozen moment they stared at each other, then Jonas struggled to get up. Avery grabbed her bag and ran from the house, slamming the door behind her. Like an answer to a prayer a taxi was letting a fare out further down the road, and she flagged it down, hurling herself inside as Jonas shot from the house so fast he went sprawling on his hands and knees.

'You all right, love?' asked the taxi driver.

'Yes, fine. Paddington Station, please,' Avery said absently, watching through the back window as Jonas picked himself up. She turned to smile into the driver's mirror. 'Don't worry; I'm not going to throw up in your cab.'

She made good her promise by sheer iron will. When she reached the station she flew down the steps to the cloakroom, fumbling with change in the turnstile in a panic, but at last managing to lock herself away in one of the lavatories before parting with everything she'd eaten for days. Retching and miserable afterwards, she eventually recovered enough to wash her face. And at last, feeling like death, she trudged up to the concourse to catch the next train home.

Avery felt numb with exhaustion when a taxi dropped her off in Gresham Road later that night. She dumped her bag down and checked her messages, unsurprised to find all of them from Jonas, demanding she ring him back. In his dreams!

She took the house phone off the hook, switched off her mobile and filled the kettle. She'd drunk several bottles of water on the train, winning strange looks from the girl in charge of the refreshment trolley, but now she needed tea, strong and hot, to bring her back to at least some semblance of life.

As the tea began its work Avery made herself a promise. She would revert to the 'no men' rule in her life and stick to it from that day forward. She smiled mirthlessly. Jonas Mercer's request for more trust on her part had been quite a joke. If he'd practised what he preached he would have waited to learn the actual facts. Instead he'd flung insults which, if only by implication, had included her mother. So to hell with him.

Next morning Avery woke up early, feeling wired and edgy. She burned off some of her nervous energy by doing twice the amount of household chores she usually did on Sundays, and afterwards drove to the nearest supermarket to lay in a week's supply of food. No lover of this form of retail therapy, Avery returned home in record time and had just started putting her supplies away when the doorbell rang.

She took the new receiver from the kitchen wall. 'Yes?'

'Avery, let me in.'

'Who is this?'

'Jonas Mercer,' he said savagely. 'As you damn well know. I need to see you.'

'If you've come to apologise—'

'I've brought your coat.'

Avery's eyes widened. She'd travelled home from London without even noticing she'd left her coat behind. It had been a bargain in Christine Porter's sale, but even with a further reduction for trade it had not been cheap. In her misery she hadn't given it a thought.

'Why didn't you just post it to me?' she said at last.

'I had nothing else planned today, and I thought you might need it. Let me in. Please.'

Oh, why not? Avery thought wearily. She might as well get it over with. She walked down the hall and opened the front door, some newfound sadistic streak taking great pleasure in Jonas's haggard appearance.

'Come into the kitchen,' she said without greeting. 'Just sling my coat over the banisters.'

Jonas stood tall and silent just inside the kitchen door, watching as Avery put food away. He looked as though he might fall down if he didn't sit down soon, she thought without sympathy.

'Would you like some coffee?' she asked.

'Thank you.'

'Do sit down,' she said politely, and filled the kettle.

Jonas pulled out a kitchen chair and let himself down gingerly. 'I saw you drive out as I turned into the other end of the road. So I waited.'

'I could have been gone for the day.'

'True. But on top of the worst hangover of my life my hands are sore, and I needed a breather before I drove back. So I waited,' he repeated. His eyes, even more bloodshot than the day before, met hers. 'I needed to talk to you.'

'If you feel as bad as you look it might have been wiser to talk on the phone,' she said coldly. She made two mugs of coffee, handed him one, and sat down at the table, facing him. 'Would you like something to eat?'

'No!' he said, shuddering. 'Thank you. Would you have answered the phone if I'd rung?'

She thought about it. 'Probably not.'

'Exactly. That's why I came.'

'I thought you came to bring my jacket.'

'As you said, I could have posted that. I came to apologise.'

'For the insult to me, or the implied one to my mother?'

Jonas flinched. 'Both.' He held out his hands, palm upwards, to show angry grazes. 'I've got knees to match. I was chasing after you to apologise, not retaliate, Avery. I regretted the words the minute they were out of my mouth. You had every right to slap me. I wanted to hit myself.'

Avery drank her coffee, unmoved.

Jonas made no move to touch his own drink. 'Will you accept my apology?'

She studied him without emotion. 'For myself I might have done, but my mother was involved so, no, I won't.'

His eyes dulled. 'I see.'

'You'd better drink your coffee,' she advised. 'You could do with a shot of caffeine.'

He shrugged. 'I don't think I could stomach it. I agreed

to the coffee to buy time, not because I had any hope of drinking it.'

Surprised by a pang of remorse, Avery opened the refrigerator and took out a small carton of orange juice. 'Perhaps vitamin C will do instead. I keep a supply of these for car journeys.'

Jonas thanked her, punched a hole in the carton with the attached straw and drained the carton in one draught. 'I was thirstier than I thought.' He gave her a look which told her what was coming next. 'Avery, I've no earthly right to ask this, but the thought of it's driving me crazy. Will you tell me what happened to the child?'

Avery's first instinct was to scream no, to tell him it was none of his business. But to be fair Paul had made it Jonas's business. 'Very well,' she said wearily. 'Because this is partly my fault. I should have known Paul Morrell would retaliate.'

He frowned. 'For what?'

Avery gave him a brief account of the episode in the garden, and won a faint, painful smile from Jonas when she described the watering-can incident. 'I ordered both Morrells to stay away from me in future and Paul left in a towering rage, obviously determined to get back at me in the worst way he could think of. He's in El Vino's most nights, so when he saw you there it saved him the trouble of contacting you to tell his little story. But he didn't tell all of it, and I can't let him get away with half-truths.' She got up to make herself more coffee, and handed Jonas another carton of orange juice.

'Contraception had always been Paul's responsibility,' she went on, looking away. 'But on this occasion his purchase must have been faulty.'

When Avery had told him she was pregnant Paul had gone berserk. He didn't want to be a father. He didn't want Avery to be a mother. She was too young. She had a brilliant career, earned such good money. And with their social life there was no place in their lives for a baby at that point. Abortion was quick and safe these days. He would pay for it, and even go with her to the clinic.

'Bloody magnanimous of him,' snarled Jonas. 'Sorry. Go on.'

'I had no intention of having an abortion,' Avery told him. 'You jumped to the wrong conclusion, Jonas. The moment I knew I was pregnant I made a conscious decision to become a single parent, like countless other women these days. My mother,' she added deliberately, 'was delighted at the thought of a grandchild.'

Jonas swallowed, looking so ill Avery asked him if he needed water. But he shook his head, motioning her to go on.

Paul had argued with Avery until she was frantic. Then a couple of weeks later she'd felt unwell all day at work, and had got home feeling too ill to go out to dinner. Shortly afterwards she'd been seized with such agonising pain she'd passed out cold, and Paul had panicked and called an ambulance.

Avery looked steadily at Jonas. 'I had an emergency laparotomy because my pregnancy was ectopic. I was bleeding into my abdomen. The affected fallopian tube was removed, and when I came round afterwards I was told there was some damage to the other tube. So no more children.'

Jonas took in a deep, unsteady breath. 'Morrell was delighted, of course,' he said bitterly.

'Positively jubilant. He told me our little problem had been solved very neatly. We would say it was an emergency appendix, and no one would be any the wiser. We could carry on as normal once I was fit.' Avery's mouth turned down. 'At that moment I was anything but fit. To Paul it was the perfect solution, but to me it was the loss of a baby. My baby. And any others I might have had. I felt ill and tearful and in desperate need of my mother, so when I was discharged Paul drove me home to Gresham Road.

'I'm ashamed to say I was too wrapped up in my own misery for a while to realise that my mother was looking worse than me. When I did I had a word with her doctor, who said her heart condition was deteriorating.' Avery got up to fetch a tissue and blew her nose. 'So I resigned my job and stayed home, not only to look after my mother and help with the work she had on hand, but to make the most of her company while I still could. I told Paul it was over between us, but he flatly refused to accept it. After all this time he still won't accept it, even though I've never let him into this house since he drove me here three years ago.'

'I could kill the bastard,' said Jonas savagely. 'I came near to it on Friday in El Vino's. After he fed me his story I took him by the throat, shook him like a rat and told him that if he breathes a word about it again I shall not only rearrange his pretty face but take great pleasure in saying he made sexual overtures to me.'

'Gosh, that should shut him up,' said Avery, impressed.

'Morrell was lucky that someone came in at that point, otherwise he might have got more than just a sore throat and a fright.' Jonas leaned forward slightly. 'His motivation is obvious. He's obviously persuaded himself that you'll relent towards him one day. Then I arrive on the scene and you tell him you're going to marry me. So the little bastard plays dirty and tries to put a stop to it.'

'And succeeds,' said Avery.

'And succeeds,' agreed Jonas harshly, straightening. He was silent for some time, but at last raised his head to lock brooding eyes with hers. 'You probably don't want to hear this right now, but I can't leave without saying it. I love you, Avery.'

She eyed him sadly. 'Yet you believed Paul. Where was that trust you talked about, Jonas?'

'I know, I know!' He rubbed a hand over his eyes. 'I wish to God I could take back what I said.'

'So do I. But you can't.' She shrugged. 'And, as Paul Morrell can testify, I'm an unforgiving soul.'

Jonas regarded her in silence for a long, tense interval that stretched Avery's nerves to breaking point. At last he nodded bleakly and stood up. 'In that case there's nothing more to say.'

Avery got to her feet, eyeing his pallor with concern. 'Are you sure you're up to the journey back so soon?'

'I'll survive. I'll call in to see my parents on the way back. I'll feign illness and let my mother fuss over me for a while.' He smiled mirthlessly, then winced. 'Damn, that hurt. My jaw is still throbbing from that slap you gave me. A good thing I don't have much to smile about right now.'

Neither had she, thought Avery, as she watched him limp down the path to his car. Jonas turned at the gate, raised a hand in sombre salute, and she closed the door quickly rather than watch him disappear out of her life.

CHAPTER ELEVEN

THREE evenings after her life-altering trip to London, Avery was about to leave for home when Nadine Cox rang.

'Great, I've caught you, Avery. I've got some flowers for you at my place. Save me a trip to Gresham Road and take them with you—there's a love.'

Avery locked up and went along to the flower shop, her eyes wide when Nadine handed over an arrangement of exquisite pink roses.

'Lovely Lady variety. Nice, aren't they? There's no note,' said Nadine, looking awkward. 'Mr Mercer ordered them, and said he would ring you to explain. If you'll take them to your car I'll carry the other bunch for you.'

'There's more?'

'I had to order the second one specially, otherwise you could have had them both yesterday,' said Nadine, and went into the back to fetch a great armful of crimson peonies. 'Treat them carefully; these babies cost a fortune. So did the roses at this time of year. By the way,' she added, 'no one else knows who sent them. Mr Mercer insisted on that, which is why I didn't come round to your place earlier.'

When Avery got home she made two trips into the house to transport her flowers to the kitchen table, then hugged her arms across her chest as she stood back to look at them. The flamboyant crimson peonies were self-explanatory, but the roses were freaking her out.

She eyed the phone, but instead of ringing Jonas she switched on the radio for company as she arranged the roses in one of her grandmother's crystal vases. But when the Walker Brothers informed her that breaking up was so very hard to do, she switched it off again. Tell me about it, she thought morosely, as she searched for a container big enough to display the peonies.

Fortunately for Avery Jonas rang her before burning curiosity had driven her to call him first. 'Did you get the flowers?' he demanded.

'Yes, indeed. Thank you. They're magnificent.'

'Was Nadine able to find red peonies?'

'She had to order them specially.'

'I noticed some in a display down here and thought of you. They're my not very original way of saying I'm sorry.'

'But why send roses as well?'

'As a useless but heartfelt apology to your mother.'

'I see.' Avery decided against telling him that pink roses had been Ellen Crawford's favourite flower. 'Are you feeling better?'

'Not much. My appearance excited considerable comment yesterday. I couldn't let on I'd been mugged by a girl, so I fixed the inquisitors with a steely look and said nothing apart from that I was feeling a bit under the weather.'

'I can picture it,' said Avery dryly. 'Thank you for ringing, Jonas. And for the flowers.'

'They may not be much consolation to you, Avery, but sending them made me feel slightly better.'

'It made me feel better, too.'

'But not to the point of a change of heart?'

'No,' she said gently. 'Not enough for that. Goodnight.'

Avery Alterations had several orders for weddings on hand; among them was Frances White's marriage to Philip Lester, who wanted his bride to wear a white wedding gown.

'I did hint that a white dress of any kind at my age could be tricky to bring off, especially in February, but in the end he persuaded me,' Frances said ruefully. 'Not that I'm going for anything over the top. I'll make a plain white sheath—

useful for dining on the honeymoon. And for the wedding I plan to wear that ecru lace jacket I bought at the antiques fair we went to last year, Avery.'

'Really?' Avery eyed her suspiciously. 'It needed a fair bit of restoration.'

'That's where you come in,' said the bride-to-be serenely, winning grins from Helen and Louise at Avery's look of dismay. 'Will you repair it for me?'

'I'd rather buy you some lace to make a new one!'

'I prefer my vintage jacket,' insisted Frances, and played her trump card. 'If someone else had brought it in you'd do it like a shot.'

Defeated, Avery promised to do her best, with the proviso that if the results failed to come up to her own exacting standard she would revert to Plan B and buy a length of ecru lace for a new jacket.

In spite of her protests Avery was grateful for the work involved in the repair. It needed such painstaking care that she took it home to concentrate on in the evenings and at the weekends, which dragged now Jonas was no longer in her life. Frances had been devastated when she heard this, but gave up asking questions when she realised Avery couldn't bear to talk about it.

The lifespan of both peonies and roses had been short, and Avery was glad of it. Every time she'd looked at the roses she heard her mother reminding her that human life was also short, and Jonas Mercer was male and human, and had been suffering from a heady mix of jealousy and disillusion laced with alcohol, and therefore not in a normal state of mind when he'd lashed out with the words that had won him a slap around the face.

Avery came to agree with this as she worked on the fragile lace. Gradually her unforgiving soul grew a lot less unforgiving, and yearned for Jonas as much as her heart did—and her body. In some ways this was the worst part of all.

She missed Jonas in ways she'd never experienced before. In the big bed she'd bought specifically to share with him she longed for him at times with an intensity that taught her it was not only the male of the species who needed cold showers in this situation. Mortified by her rampaging hormones, she took to watching the television he'd given her instead of lying awake all night aching for him.

'Avery, you look exhausted,' said Frances one afternoon, when Louise and Helen had left for the day. 'I'm sorry now that I asked you to mend the jacket. I could have copied it easily enough.'

'My problem is insomnia, not your jacket,' Avery assured her.

'And Jonas is the cause of the insomnia?'

'Who else?'

Frances went on with the seam she was sewing, but after a while she looked up, her blue eyes gentle. 'What went wrong, love?'

Avery told her tale as briefly and unemotionally as possible. 'The thing is,' she said at last, 'I was so high and mighty about it. Now I'm in a more rational frame of mind I know that my mother would tell me to forgive and forget.'

'Then tell Jonas that.'

'I can't do that!'

'Why?'

'Pride.'

'Which is making you unhappy,' said her friend bluntly. 'Ring him tonight.'

'I'm going to a Chamber of Trade meeting tonight,' said Avery promptly.

Frances rolled her big blue eyes. 'That won't take all night. Ring him when you get home.'

Avery went to her meeting, joined the others for a drink in the Angel afterwards, then went home to check her phone as usual. And as usual there was no message from Jonas. Not that she had expected one.

She spent next morning on the road, driving to appointments for fittings, and got back in time for lunch to find Frances waiting impatiently for her.

'We had someone in this morning asking for a repair to a dress.'

'Not unusual. That's what I do. What's the problem?'

'She'd like it back tomorrow.' Frances produced a black silk dress with a label which made Avery's mouth water. Frances turned it inside out and pointed to the place where a few inches of the side seam had come undone. 'Only it hasn't *come* undone, exactly. The stitches have been snipped with a scissors.'

Avery frowned. 'Was the lady trying to let it out a bit, do you think?'

'I doubt it. She looked pretty slim to me. But she was in such a rush she forgot to leave her name.'

'Odd. OK. I'll do it straight after lunch, before I start the embroidery on Tracey Barrett's wedding dress.'

'Did you make that phone call last night?' asked Frances.

'No. I told you. I had a meeting to go to, and we had a drink afterwards.'

'I see. What excuse have you thought up for tonight?'

Avery's chin lifted. 'Look, Frances, you might as well know I'm not going to ring Jonas tonight or any other night. It's over.'

Frances eyed her in deep dismay, but something about Avery's manner discouraged argument. She held up her hands in rueful surrender. 'All right. You're the boss. I won't nag you any more.'

The owner of the silk dress arrived in the shop next day, just after Philip had taken Frances out for lunch, and Avery took one look at the fair hair and ravishingly beautiful face and knew exactly who she was.

The young woman smiled, her eyes frankly curious. 'Hello. Are you Avery Crawford? I'm Hetty Tremayne.'

'I know.'

'Really?'

Aware of interest from Helen and Louise, Avery introduced them and then produced the dress to display the invisible repair.

'Marvellous!' said its owner. 'Good as new. How much do I owe you?'

Avery named the lowest sum she could possibly charge for the simple repair, money was handed over and change returned, and Hetty Tremayne smiled coaxingly.

'You know I live a fair distance away? I need a bite to eat before I start back, so as thanks for doing the repair so quickly please let me buy you lunch.'

'That's very kind of you. Thank you.'

On the short walk to the café Hetty smiled apologetically. 'I was afraid to leave my name yesterday in case you wouldn't see me.'

Avery shook her head. 'No danger of that. But if you'd wanted to talk to me we could have had lunch without injury to the dress.'

'I wasn't sure you'd agree to that,' explained Hetty, oblivious of heads turning as they entered the café. Her waxed jacket had seen as much service as her yellow cable sweater and leather brogues, but the face and irresistible smile drew every eye in the place as she made for a table at the back, where a slim, fair man got to his feet as Hetty led Avery towards him.

'How do you do? I'm Charlie Tremayne.'

'I know,' said Avery, smiling, and took his hand. 'I've seen your photograph.'

'Sorry to spring Charlie on you,' said Hetty, 'but I was afraid you'd draw the line at two of us.'

Charlie held a chair for Avery, and looked at her with

frank interest as the three of them settled at the table. 'It's good of you to spare the time to see us.'

'Is something wrong?' she asked, looking from the pleasant, unremarkable face to the traffic-stopping features of his wife.

'Yes, it is,' said Hetty gloomily. 'But let's order first. What do you recommend? And I know today's special is meat and potato pie, Charlie, but please give it a miss. We have that all the time at home.'

While they waited for toasted sandwiches the Tremaynes asked interested questions about Avery's business, leaving the real reason for their visit until their lunch arrived.

'I'm delighted to meet you both, but why did you want to see me?' asked Avery as she took a sandwich.

Hetty sighed. 'We both love Jonas is the short answer. We just can't stand by and do nothing when he's making such a pig's breakfast of his life.'

Avery sat suddenly still. 'What's wrong?'

Charlie gave her a worried frown. 'Jonas does nothing but work, work, work. He won't come to the Barn, he won't go to Lilian for Sunday lunch—'

'Who's Lilian?'

'His mother. She's worried. I am too.'

Hetty nodded in agreement. 'Jonas is in imminent danger of becoming a statistic. I can just see the headlines.'

Avery blinked. 'What headlines?'

'You know the kind of thing—"Thirty-something entrepreneur dies from coronary through overwork". Are you prepared to let him do that?' demanded Hetty as she filled their cups.

'It's not up to me. I haven't seen Jonas for ages—'

'That's the point,' said Charlie gently. 'You sent him packing and he's taking it hard.'

Avery stirred her coffee slowly. 'So what do you want me to do?'

'For starters, tell us why you won't forgive him.'

She looked up sharply. 'Jonas told you I won't?'

Charlie shook his head. 'Lilian rang me, asking for help, so I went charging off to London to see him. I practically had to apply thumbscrews to make Jonas talk, but in the end he told me you won't marry him. He wouldn't say why.'

Hetty leaned nearer. 'Tell us the truth, darling. Do you love Jonas?'

Avery thought about lying, but in the end nodded reluctantly. 'Yes. I do.'

'Then can't you tell him that? Charlie says Jonas is crazy about you. So kiss and make up, Avery. Please.'

'I've known him since we were both thirteen,' said Charlie heavily, 'and I've never seen him like this before.'

Hetty took Avery's hand. 'One phone call is all it would take. Then the next time you come to the Barn the four of us can celebrate.'

Avery smiled wryly. 'Does Jonas bring all his girlfriends to meet the Tremaynes?'

'No,' said Charlie, and kissed her on both cheeks as they parted outside the café. 'You'll be the first, Avery.'

The Tremaynes drove off, plainly satisfied that they'd done something to help Jonas, but Avery went back to work feeling guilty. She had actually promised nothing. She had no intention of getting in touch with Jonas, no matter what Hetty said about coronaries.

Avery handed over the lace jacket next day. 'I hope it will do, Frances. Speak now if it won't, because we've got just three days to make another one.'

'It's perfect,' said Frances, examining it, her smile so luminous Avery relaxed.

'That's pretty miraculous, boss,' said Helen, inspecting the lace closely. 'How on earth do you do it?'

'Very slowly!'

'I never thought you'd manage it,' said Louise frankly.

'I knew she would.' Frances smiled serenely. 'I had complete faith in Avery's magic.'

The day of the wedding dawned bitterly cold and grey, but by the afternoon February had relented and a wintry sun came out in good time for the ceremony. Avery arrived early, with Helen and Louise and their husbands, and sat towards the front of the candlelit church, admiring the flowers Nadine had arranged with her usual artistry.

Philip, usually the calmest of men, sat fidgeting beside his best man, looking as nervous as a first-time bridegroom, and a young woman in a ravishing hat leant over the pew to whisper encouragement and give him a kiss. On the stroke of two the organ began the wedding march and Frances, radiant in her white dress and elegant lace jacket, came down the aisle on her father's arm, followed by Philip's beaming seven-year-old granddaughter in sapphire-blue velvet.

'Frances looks so elegant,' whispered Helen beside her. 'I can see why she wanted to wear that jacket.'

The ceremony had ended and the smiling bride and groom were halfway down the aisle to the strains of Wagner before Avery discovered a familiar figure standing a few pews behind her, and she promptly dropped her small black clutch purse to give herself time to recover.

Frances had made no mention of inviting Jonas.

Outside in the cold winter sunshine there was the usual photo shoot, which included the bride's request for an Avery Alterations group photograph. When Avery took her place next to Frances, with Helen and Louise on either side, she was burningly conscious of Jonas, but he seemed unaware of her as he talked to Tom Bennett and Andy Collins.

'You were pretty secretive about the guest-list,' she muttered to the bride, and Frances smiled, unrepentant.

'So sue me. It's my wedding. You can't be cross with me today.'

'Smile!' ordered the photographer.

When the photo shoot was over, and the bride and groom had driven off to the reception, Jonas finally came to join Avery.

'Hello,' she said, smiling brightly. 'I didn't know you were coming.'

'Frances advised against telling you in advance.' His answering smile was cool. 'Would you have developed a mysterious illness if you'd known?'

'And spoil the bride's day? Of course not.'

'You look beautiful,' he said quietly.

Avery had bought a white wool jacket from Christine to wear with the black dress Jonas had once described as plain and perfect. She'd pulled her hair back into its usual severe twist, but softened the effect with a frivolous trifle of a black hat decorated with waving fronds.

'You look good, too,' she returned.

He gave her a mocking smile as cars began to leave. 'Tom said there was no point in packing five of you into his car, so he asked me to chauffeur you to the Angel. Is that all right with you?'

'Of course. Thank you.' Avery smiled frostily. 'These shoes weren't made for walking.'

The drive was short, and the atmosphere so constrained in the car that Avery yearned to switch the radio on to compensate for the lack of conversation. When they arrived at the Angel Avery hurried through the hotel foyer to the small private dining room hired for the occasion, and pinned on a bright smile as they went inside. She threw her arms round Frances and kissed her affectionately.

'Be happy, Mrs Lester. Congratulations, Mr Lester.' She kissed Philip in turn, Jonas added his own congratulations, and after introductions to each set of parents Avery suggested they join Helen and Louise and their husbands. She felt quite proud of herself as she sipped champagne and talked and laughed so normally with the others she felt she deserved an Oscar.

Philip and Frances had invited so few guests it was more like an intimate party than a wedding reception, and although Jonas had to field questions about the progress of the cinema complex at first, eventually he made it clear he preferred to pay attention to Philip's daughter Verity, on one side, and Avery, on the other. Speeches were made and toasts drunk, and after the cake had been cut the bride and groom came to talk to everyone in turn, both of them so obviously happy Avery felt a pang of envy as she laughed and chatted with her friend and teased her about being an instant grandma.

'She doesn't look the part, does she?' agreed Verity, laughing. 'Lucy thinks it's so cool to have a grandma she calls by her first name.'

In the foyer later, after the bride and groom had been seen off for the first stage of their trip in a shower of rice and confetti, Avery turned to Helen and Louise with a rueful smile.

'Weddings are tiring.'

'But it's too early to go home; come and have a drink in the bar—unless you've got a better offer,' whispered Helen as Jonas came towards them.

'Avery, do you need a lift home?' he asked. 'I'm driving back to London.'

'You're going back tonight?' she said, surprised.

'Afraid so.'

'Then, thank you. I was just about to call a taxi.'

After a round of leave-taking they finally emerged, shivering, into an icy wind that threatened Avery's hat.

'The wedding invitation came as quite a surprise,' said

Jonas, as he saw her into his car. 'I need your advice on a suitable present.'

'Tricky with a second marriage,' said Avery, grateful for a topic of conversation. 'Philip's a barbecue man in the summer, so maybe some new garden furniture, or a big stone pot with an unusual plant. If you like I'll consult Frances when she gets back and let you know.'

'You're actually volunteering to communicate with me?' he asked, in a tone which silenced Avery very effectively for the rest of the journey.

When they arrived at the house he surprised her by turning into the drive instead of parking in the road. He gave her a mocking smile as he switched off the ignition.

'You'd better ask me in, otherwise all Frances's efforts to play Cupid will have been in vain. Or do I mean Fairy Godmother?'

'I rather think that's the Tremaynes' role,' said Avery, startling him. 'Come in if you want.'

She ran to the front door, hanging on to her hat in a wind that felt as though it came straight from Siberia. Once inside the house she unpinned the feather-trimmed scrap of velvet and put it in the tissue-lined hatbox lying open on the hall table.

'I hired the hat for the occasion,' she explained as Jonas closed the door behind him. 'It goes back in the morning.'

'Never mind the hat. What's this about the Tremaynes?'

'I'll explain after I've made tea—or would you prefer coffee?' asked Avery. 'I'd better not offer you a drink if you're driving.'

'I don't want anything,' he said impatiently.

'Come in here, then.' She led him into the study, pulling a face as a sudden fusillade of rain battered the French windows. 'Frances was lucky this held off until now. Your drive home won't be very pleasant.'

'I'll cope,' he said, shrugging.

'Excuse me for a moment, I won't be long,' said Avery. She ran upstairs to exchange her jacket for a thick scarlet cardigan and shivered as the wind hurled icy rain against the windows. She wished now that she'd come home alone by taxi when she'd had the chance, instead of coping with Jonas Mercer in his present mood. When she steeled herself to go downstairs again he was slumped in a corner of the sofa, staring into the unlit fire. He got up punctiliously as she went in the room, but she waved him back to his seat and took the other corner of the sofa, making a note to invest in a new chair soon to avoid intimacy of this kind in future.

'Are you sure I can't give you some coffee?' she said politely.

Jonas eyed her coldly. 'No, Avery. I want to know what the hell you meant about the Tremaynes.'

'Hetty came to my shop to get a dress repaired, but that was just an excuse to meet me,' she began, and told him the entire story.

Jonas heard her out in silence, his face inscrutable. When Avery came to a stop he smiled derisively. 'Hetty and Charlie, not to mention my lady mother, have been remarkably busy on my behalf. Busy, but unsuccessful,' he added. 'If the Tremaynes asked you to contact me they failed in their mission.'

Avery shrugged. 'I didn't promise anything. After all, it's been a long time since we last spoke, Jonas. I assumed you'd—well, moved on.'

'Moved on?' he repeated without inflection. 'That's not far wrong, I suppose. A man can only grovel so much. You made it clear last time we spoke that nothing I could say or do would put things right between us.'

'So why did you come to the wedding?' she demanded.

'To please Frances,' he informed her, deflating her very effectively. 'I came to make sure nothing spoiled her wedding day.'

Avery raised a supercilious eyebrow. 'Why would your absence do that?'

'Frances enclosed a note with her invitation, saying it would be good for Avery to have a friend for company at the reception. The tone of the note made it plain that Frances wanted that very much, even if you didn't, so I accepted the invitation.'

So Jonas hadn't come in the hope of reconciliation today, after all. 'It was very good of you to spare the time,' said Avery, flinching as another onslaught battered the windows.

'By the sound of it I'd better be on my way.' Jonas got up.

Avery hugged the cardigan round her as she preceded him out of the room. In unbroken silence they walked the length of the hall, but when Avery opened the front door Jonas swore volubly and they looked out into a wild, white night. A layer of hail had blown into the porch and now snow was falling in a thick, obliterating curtain, driven across the garden by the rising wind.

'That was hail we heard, not rain,' said Avery, and slammed the door shut. 'Now it's turned to a blizzard. You can't possibly drive to London in this weather, so you'd better stay the night. Don't worry,' she added, 'I'm not trying to lure you into my bed.'

'I didn't think so for a moment,' he said suavely. 'I don't jump to conclusions any more.'

Their eyes met and held for a moment. 'You can sleep in the spare room at the front,' said Avery at last.

'Thank you.' He smiled for the first time since their arrival. 'I've offered to often enough before.'

She nodded briskly. 'But it's early yet. Let's have something to eat. I'm hungry.'

'You ate so little at the reception I'm not surprised. My presence was the appetite depressant, I assume?'

'Not at all. It was the chef's way with local salmon. I

prefer mine out of a tin. But that's a deadly secret,' she warned lightly.

Jonas looked amused. 'I won't rat on you.'

Feeling a little easier, Avery went towards the kitchen. 'Perhaps you'd put a match to the fire while I throw some sandwiches together.'

She worked quickly, not sure whether she was grateful or sorry for the quirk of fate that had handed her this unexpected time with Jonas. When she'd turned to see him in the church her heart had missed a beat and she'd taken it for granted, right up to a few minutes ago, that he'd accepted the invitation just to meet up with her again. She'd even prepared a graceful little speech, informing him that if he'd come on her account his mission had been in vain. But Jonas had come for no other reason than to please Frances. Whatever the Tremaynes might think, he was working hard because he enjoyed doing it, or the job demanded it, or for any number of reasons other than languishing over Avery Crawford.

CHAPTER TWELVE

THE constraint between them gradually eased as they ate supper in front of the fire. The conversation centred on the wedding during the meal, but when Avery handed Jonas a mug of coffee afterwards she took the bull by the horns.

'You're angry with me.'

He shook his head. 'With myself, not you, Avery. I could have answered Frances with a polite little note of regret, asked Hannah to order some expensive trifle as a present—'

'Who's Hannah?'

'I inherited her from my father. She's my assistant.' Jonas turned to look at her, his eyes glittering between the spiky lashes. 'Not the new woman in my life, unfortunately.'

'Why? Doesn't she like you?'

'Hannah is almost old enough to be my mother and has a husband and two teenage sons. She's also so efficient I'd go down on my knees and beg if she tried to resign.'

'Oh.'

'I said *unfortunately*,' he repeated with emphasis, 'because I don't have a new woman in my life. You were a hard act to follow. But,' he added, before Avery could say anything, 'life's been too hectic to waste it on useless regrets. Like a sensible chap I knuckled down to the clean break you're so fond of. Then like a fool I turned up to the wedding today.'

'You made Frances happy,' said Avery quietly. 'And until she comes back from Barbados she won't know that her stratagem failed.'

Jonas gazed moodily into the fire. 'I was doing fine until

170

I saw you today. I'd persuaded myself I didn't want you any more, but one look and I knew I'd been fooling myself. God knows why,' he added, eyeing her moodily. 'It's bloody hard work trying to have a relationship with you, and with your hair scraped back like that you're not even beautiful.'

'Compared with Hetty Tremayne I'm a complete turn-off,' agreed Avery tartly.

'Not to me, more's the pity. Tell me the truth, Avery,' he asked abruptly, 'have you thawed towards me?'

She nodded slowly. 'Yes.'

'How much?'

'Completely.'

'Then why the hell didn't you get in touch?'

'Why the hell didn't you?' she snapped.

He glared at her. 'You told me to get lost!'

Avery backed down. 'I intended to ring you. I had Frances pressuring me to do it, as well as Hetty Tremayne. But in the end I decided against it. Same old reasons.'

'Oh, God, are we back to the subject of progeny again?'

'Afraid so.' Avery got up. 'I'm off to put sheets on the spare bed.'

'Can I help?'

'No, thanks. I can manage.'

'Tell me something I don't know,' he said wearily.

Avery collected linen and towels from the airing cupboard and drew the curtains in the spare room to shut out the howling white night. She made up the bed and went downstairs again, and heard Jonas talking on his cellphone in the study. She backed out hurriedly and retreated to the kitchen, wishing vainly that they could go back to the brief, halcyon period of their relationship before Paul's deliberate malice had ruined everything.

When Avery returned to the study Jonas was in his former

place on the sofa. He retracted his long legs for her to pass him, and she sat down again in her corner.

'The bed's done, and I've put towels and a spare tooth-brush in the bathroom,' she informed him.

Jonas eyed her quizzically. 'Efficient! Even to the spare toothbrush ready for unexpected male guests.'

'I don't have male guests, but I always have spare tooth-brushes. I just can't resist "three for the price of two" offers in the Stow Street chemist,' she told him, unmoved.

'I'm glad,' he said soberly.

'That I have spare toothbrushes?'

'That I'm the only man to enjoy a sleepover here.'

'You don't appear to be enjoying this one very much!'

He smiled crookedly. 'You're wrong there. I'm just too bloody-minded to show it. That was my mother on the phone, by the way. Dad heard about the weather conditions up here. She was very relieved when I told her I was staying the night.'

'Did you say where?'

Jonas shook his head. 'No point in getting her hopes up. Hetty's probably described you to her in detail by now. If Mother knew I was sleeping here tonight she'd start listening for the patter of tiny feet.'

Avery turned away sharply, and Jonas put a hand out to touch hers.

'Sorry. I'm a tactless swine.'

She shrugged. 'No point in pussyfooting around the subject.'

He sat staring at his shoes for some time, and then turned to look at her. 'Avery.'

She tensed, her antennae instantly erect. 'Yes?'

'I've done a lot of thinking over the past few weeks. Mainly at night,' he admitted. 'Mercom takes up all my waking hours.'

'So Charlie Tremayne said.'

'He means well.'

'I know.'

The dark-fringed eyes locked with hers. 'Do you want to hear the conclusion to all this thinking?'

Avery licked her tongue round suddenly dry lips. 'I'm not sure that I do,' she said warily.

'It's perfectly simple. We adopt a child. More than one, if you want—'

'No!' She shook her head vehemently.

Jonas remained surprisingly calm. 'Does that mean you don't want to adopt, or that the things I said—and immediately regretted—are still a barrier between us?'

'I flew off the handle at first, but I'm over the second bit now.'

'Is that the truth?'

'Gospel,' she assured him.

'Then it's the adoption you can't agree to?'

'Yes.'

'So it's back to square one.' He sat silent for a while, his eyes on the flames. 'I lied, Avery,' he said abruptly.

'About what?'

He turned to look at her. 'I turned up today with the express purpose of seeing *you*. I knew damn well I'd been invited as your partner. And to keep Frances happy I knew you'd have to play along.'

She eyed him militantly. 'If you came just to see me you didn't show it!'

'Because the moment I saw you again I was furious about the time we're wasting apart. Instead of kissing you senseless I wanted to wring your neck.' He gave her the sudden, bone-dissolving smile which kept her awake at night. 'Guess which one I want to do right now.'

Avery scrambled to her feet, warding him off as he leapt up to join her. 'No, Jonas. There's no point. You could kiss me, and I'd kiss you back and so on, but afterwards we'd still be at square one.'

He stood back. 'You're right,' he said promptly, taking the wind out of her sails.

Her response had been knee-jerk retaliation for his attitude earlier on. But he could have tried a bit harder, she thought resentfully, and turned away to rake the fire to ashes. 'You go on up. I'll see to the alarm and the lights.'

'Right. I'll see you in the morning, then,' Jonas said casually. 'Goodnight.'

Avery stared blankly at his back view as he left the room. Crestfallen, she went through her usual security routine, taking more time over it than usual, before she went upstairs. She paused at the top, heard water running in the bathroom and tiptoed along the landing to her room. Feeling edgy and restless, and scornful because she knew perfectly well why, she undressed and ran a hot bath fragrant with the lavender and rosemary bath oil which was supposed to help her sleep.

The aromatherapy failed miserably. It was strange, Avery thought much later, that one could be snug in a warm, comfortable bed and feel desperately tired, yet stay wide awake. She tossed and turned, and then tensed, heart pounding and eyes tightly shut, as the door opened. She heard it close and took in a deep breath, then let it out in a rush as a naked male body slid into bed beside her.

'I want you so much I can't sleep,' growled Jonas as he took her in his arms.

'What took you so long?' she whispered back, and he gave a smothered laugh, then kissed her, his hands exploring.

'You forgot to undress,' he accused.

'I'm wearing the red pyjamas I bought myself for Christmas.'

'Not any more,' he said huskily, his long hands clumsy for once in his haste to get her naked.

Avery helped him eagerly, savouring the touch and taste and smell of him as they held each other close for a long, relishing moment. Then Jonas reached out an arm to switch on the bedside lamp and propped himself up on an elbow to look down into her face.

'I've lain awake night after night imagining this,' he told her, smoothing tumbled hair back from her forehead. 'I have to make sure you're real.'

Avery smiled luminously. 'There are other ways to make sure.'

'Thinking about them causes the insomnia!' He switched off the light and kissed her.

The kiss was long and slow, his teeth nibbling gently at her lips, his tongue teasing hers, seducing it, his hands moving over her body as though he meant to memorise its shape by touch. When his hands cupped her breasts they tightened in anticipation, and she caught her breath as his lips and clever, relentless fingertips sent lightning bolts of sensation through her body down to the place that grew hot and liquid in response. His hands and mouth moved lower in caresses which heightened their mutual arousal to fever-pitch. When he parted her thighs at last she tensed in eager anticipation, expecting him to slide up and over her and plunge himself into her waiting heat. Instead she felt the touch of his lips on her scar, and then the delicious torment of his dividing, probing tongue as it brought her to gasping, helpless release.

Jonas slid up to hold her close in his arms and Avery buried her hot, damp face against him.

'I didn't want that to happen,' she protested hoarsely.

'Didn't you like it?' he teased.

'Not much point in saying no!' She rubbed her cheek against skin. 'But I would have preferred it with you inside me.'

He breathed in sharply, and she felt his erection nudge

against her. 'That can be arranged,' he said with difficulty as she slid her hand down to investigate.

'Now, please?' Avery asked, and then gave a deep, visceral moan of pleasure as he sheathed himself to the hilt inside her. After the deprivation of time spent apart they moved together with such passionate need that climax quickly overtook Avery again, but this time Jonas was with her, part of her, his mouth crushing hers as they shared the final rapture.

They fell asleep at once, held close in each other's arms. When Avery woke it was early morning and she was still held fast by a possessive arm and a long, confining leg. She smiled in sleepy approval at the ceiling, which looked so white it was obvious what kind of day waited outside. She must get up and look soon, but it could wait a little longer. Because Jonas was so warm and she was so comfortable…

When Avery woke again she was alone. The curtains were drawn back to reveal a winter wonderland outside and she could hear Jonas whistling in her shower. She slid out of bed and scrambled into the red pyjamas he'd tossed across the room the night before. While she was struggling with her hair Jonas appeared in the doorway with a towel slung round his hips, so obviously trying not to laugh at the sight of her that Avery shied a pillow at him.

'Temper, temper,' he said, wagging his finger at her.

'Don't laugh at my pyjamas, then,' she said tartly. She pulled on her dressing gown and went to the window to look at the snow-covered garden. 'Wow!' she said with awe. 'I bet that's put paid to the camellia.'

'Never mind the damned camellia—think of my car! I hope you keep a shovel handy,' he said, coming to stand behind her, but Avery slid away from his grasp.

'I'll have a shower now my bathroom's available,' she said quickly.

Jonas took her by the shoulders, his face stern. 'Avery,

after last night there's no point in trying to shift us back to square one.'

'I know.' She grinned as his eyes flickered.

'You're agreeing with me?'

'Yes.' She drew a hand down his flat-muscled torso. 'You're freezing. Go and dress while I shower, and we'll talk over breakfast.'

Avery went downstairs twenty minutes later, wearing her scarlet cardigan over black wool sweater and trousers, and found Jonas shivering in shirtsleeves as he put down his phone. He eyed her enviously.

'You look warm, darling. I've just rung my father and told him I can't make it today. He'll take over until I get back.'

'So you're stuck here with me,' she said, delighted, and eyed him with sympathy. 'You must be so cold! I'll see what I can find.'

Avery went upstairs to rummage through her wardrobe and returned to the kitchen holding out a heavy grey jersey. 'Lucky for you I tend to buy men's sweaters for the length. Try this.'

On Jonas the garment was too snug round the chest, and an inch or two shorter than he would have liked. 'But it's warm,' he said gratefully, and kissed her. 'Thank you, darling. What's for breakfast?'

While Jonas cut bread and made the tea Avery had requested instead of coffee, she made a vast omelette. They fell on the food like wolves, so hungry they were at the toast and marmalade stage before making any attempt at serious discussion.

'Now we talk,' said Jonas as Avery poured tea. 'So, Ms Crawford, where do we go from here?'

'I vote we backtrack a bit—not to square one,' she said hastily at the black look he threw her. 'Let's rewind to the time before Paul did his dirty work.'

'You mean you want a part-time lover again?' he said, resigned.

'For now, yes.'

'For now,' he repeated thoughtfully. 'What does that mean?'

'We get used to being together again.'

'We won't be together much!'

'It's better than the alternative. Maybe you can make it to the Barn on special occasions, and I'll come down to London every weekend I can,' she promised.

He eyed her sombrely. 'I was afraid you'd never set foot in my house again.'

She gave him a wry little smile. 'I could use a warmer welcome next time I come!'

'Guaranteed.' Jonas leaned nearer. 'Talking of welcomes, I couldn't even get you to kiss me downstairs last night, so it was a pretty wild gamble to get into your bed stark naked later on.'

Avery grinned. 'I'd been lying awake for ages, hoping you'd come.'

'Then why the devil didn't you come creeping into my bed?' he demanded.

She shook her head. 'I'm all for equality of the sexes, but this was definitely your move. You'd been pretty hostile earlier on. If I'd come to you—wearing those red pyjamas, remember?—for all I knew you might have told me to get lost.'

Jonas eyed her scornfully. 'As scenarios go that's the most unlikely I've ever heard.' He got up and went round the table to pull her to her feet. 'Take it from me, Avery Crawford, any time you come creeping into my bed I'll be ready and waiting—just like this.' He wrapped his arms round her and gave her the kind of long, slow kiss that led to a lot more of the same, and in the end she had to tear herself away to ring Helen and Louise.

Avery confirmed that the shop would be closed for the day, received assurances from both of them that they'd work extra hours as soon as it reopened, had a little chat about the wedding each time, then put the phone down and with a smile turned to Jonas, holding out her arms. 'Where were we?'

Much to their mutual regret a thaw set in by late morning. The sun came out after lunch, and the temperature rose to what the television weather forecaster described as 'near the seasonal normal', and the problem of the car was solved without recourse to a shovel.

'I'll have to go in the morning,' said Jonas, as they lay curled together in front of the fire after lunch. 'A pity the snow didn't hang on a bit longer.'

'We've got the rest of the day,' said Avery drowsily.

'And the night,' he reminded her. 'So, tell me, what did you think of my London house?'

'I wasn't there long enough to look at it properly, but it's the last type of house I'd expected you to own because it's so ultra-conventional.' She gave him a wry look. 'I didn't see much of it. My attention was on the drunk and dangerous owner.'

His eyes gleamed and he touched a finger to his mouth. 'You were the dangerous one, Avery Crawford. That was one stinging slap.'

'Sorry about that— No,' she corrected herself, 'I'm not sorry. You said what you said, and I did what I did, so we'll call it quits.'

'Which is only fair,' he said soberly. 'Anyway, my parents decided to go for something smaller and more modern a couple of years ago, and almost as an afterthought asked if I wanted to take on the family home. To their surprise— and mine—I liked the idea. So I sold my flat and moved in.' He turned her face up to his. 'When the "for now" period is over, could you live there with me, Avery?'

'As far as the house is concerned I could,' she said cautiously. 'But living together is a big step. We haven't known each other very long, Jonas.'

'Long enough for me to fall hopelessly in love with you.' He kissed her to underline his statement.

'Not hopelessly at all,' she said breathlessly, when she could speak. 'I feel the same about you.'

'Thank God for that! So when will you come and live with me?'

'After Frances comes back, and I've tidied up a few loose ends. If we're still together—'

'Damn right we'll be together,' said Jonas sternly, and cupped her face in his hands. 'I'm never going to let you get away again. So learn to live with that, Avery Crawford.'

Three weeks later Jonas arrived in Gresham Road just before dark on a Friday night, and drove Avery to the Barn for the weekend.

'At last,' he said with a sigh, as they bumped over the cattle grids on the way to the house, which stood out like a lighthouse in the dark. 'I see Hetty's insisted on illuminations. A pity Charlie isn't footing the electricity bill.'

'Scrooge!' said Avery, laughing. 'Are they likely to be inside, waiting for us?'

'No. Charlie was all for that, but Hetty told him you'd probably want to go straight to bed. Do you?' he added as the car came to a halt.

'Only if you're coming too!'

'That's definitely my plan. But if you're very good I may allow you a little light refreshment first.'

'I hope it's not too light. I'm starving.'

Jonas unlocked the door and Avery wandered happily round the great room, touching the winged lion as she renewed her acquaintance with the frieze of ancient cavalrymen over the fireplace. 'At one point I thought I'd never come here again,' she said, turning to Jonas.

He took her in his arms and held her tightly. 'We shouldn't be here now. We should be down in London, talking about the changes you want made to the house.' His eyes narrowed. 'Unless you've changed your mind about living in Chiswick?'

'Of course I haven't,' she said tartly, then bit her lip. 'Sorry. I sound like a nagging wife.'

'I wish you were. The wife bit, I mean. Come on,' he said briskly, taking her hand. 'Let's see what we can do about supper.'

'Shall I help you get things in from the car?'

'I didn't bring any food.'

'Jonas!' she wailed. 'Tell me you don't mean that.'

He laughed and led her into the kitchen. 'Hetty and Mrs Holmes did the catering.'

Avery gave a gusty sigh of pleasure as she saw the platter of chicken salad keeping company with a familiar pie on the table. A note signed 'H & C', followed by a row of kisses, informed them that the fridge was full and two loaves of Mrs Holmes's special bread were in the crock.

They ate supper at the kitchen table, but Avery waited until they were sitting in front of the fire together afterwards before telling him why she'd requested this weekend at the Barn instead of going down to Chiswick.

'I've been unusually busy this week, Jonas,' she began, and detached herself from his encircling arm.

He eyed her warily. 'Why can't I hold you while you tell me about it?'

'After being parted from you for a week, it tends to slow my thinking processes.'

'Does it?' he said, so smugly delighted Avery gave him a punch on his shoulder.

'Yes. So keep your distance for a bit. And,' she added severely, 'don't look at me like that, either.'

His eyes widened innocently. 'Like what?'

'You know perfectly well! So, listen. I'm trying to tell you that the "for now" period is over.'

Jonas was suddenly still. 'What exactly are you saying?' he asked carefully.

'Nothing ominous,' she assured him, her smile so radiant that life came back to his face. 'I'll move into your big conventional house as soon as you like. If you still want me.'

Jonas pulled her into his arms and held her tightly, rubbing his cheek against hers. 'Of course I still want you, woman. Let's go to bed.'

'Not so fast,' she scolded, pulling away. 'I haven't told you about my busy week yet.'

With a sigh Jonas released her and sat back, arms folded. 'There. I'm all ears, so fire away.'

'I invited Frances and Philip round for dinner on Monday evening—'

'You told me that on the phone.'

'True, but I didn't tell you why.' Avery smiled triumphantly. 'I asked Frances how she'd feel about taking over the business.'

Jonas shot upright 'Did you, indeed! What did she say?'

'She's all for it. So is Philip. He's happy to deal with the financial side, and Frances plans to advertise for someone to replace me.'

'She'll have a problem with that, darling.' Jonas kissed her swiftly. 'You're one of a kind.'

'So you told me! Anyway, next day we told Helen and Louise, who were rather sweet about missing me when I go, but so relieved to keep their jobs they promised to give Frances all the support they can.' Avery tucked a tress of hair behind her ear and took in a deep breath. 'Next day an estate agent—*not* George Morrell—had a look round my house and named a price about twice as much as I expected.'

Jonas got up, pulled her to her feet, and then sat down again with her in his lap. 'After that I insist on holding on to you, Avery Crawford. Your thought processes will just have to put up with it.'

She wriggled closer. 'Actually, I need you close to give you the next piece of news.'

His arms tightened. 'So what other little bombshell have you got for me?'

Avery took in a deep breath. 'I'm two weeks past the end of the first trimester. I've made it past the tricky stage. I can hardly believe it yet, but I'm well and truly pregnant. We're having a baby, Jonas.'

He stared at her, utterly dumbfounded. 'But, my darling girl, how?'

She bubbled over with laughter. 'You know how, Jonas Mercer.'

He kissed her fiercely, then raised his head to look down at her in wonder. 'But I thought you couldn't—'

'I was told I couldn't. But I'd never put it to the test until I met you.'

'My God, that's utterly amazing!' Jonas smiled so triumphantly that tears of joy filled Avery's eyes. 'When did you know?' he demanded, kissing the tears away.

She sniffed inelegantly. 'My system has been irregular ever since the laparotomy, so I didn't take much notice when the usual signs failed to appear. By the time I did find out you and I weren't friends any more.'

He snorted. 'That's one way of putting it! But why in God's name didn't you let me know?'

'Pride,' she said simply. 'You would have taken it for granted I was asking you to marry me.'

'Which I would have done,' Jonas said with emphasis.

'I know that! But I wanted us to get back together because you *wanted* to, not because you felt you had to. Besides, I was terrified I'd have another ectopic pregnancy, or something else would go wrong. With my medical history I was told to be careful until after the third month, so I forced myself to wait until it was safe before giving you the glad news.' Avery smiled up at him. 'Now you know why I was against adoption.'

He shook his head, looking bemused. 'And you've kept this to yourself all this time?'

'It wasn't easy, believe me! But I had to be sure.' She breathed in deeply, her eyes steady on his. 'So, can I ask you a question, Jonas?'

'As many as you like.'

'Just one. Will you marry me?'

He gave a shout of triumph. 'The minute I can get a special licence,' he said huskily, and kissed her with a tenderness which brought the tears back as he set her very carefully on her feet.

'It's all right, darling, I'm as healthy as a horse!' she protested, sniffing.

He ran a loving hand over her tumbled mane of hair. 'My thoroughbred,' he said huskily. 'We're invited to lunch over at the house with Hetty and Charlie tomorrow. Shall we give them the news?'

'Of course. Ask Charlie to be your best man first, then tell them we'll need some godparents in six months' time!'

An invitation to the afternoon reception thrown to celebrate the autumn opening of the Stow Street cinema complex was the hottest ticket in town. On the big day, among palms and flower arrangements provided by Cox Flowers, champagne and canapés were served in the foyer to a crowd of guests—some of whom were there in an official capacity, to represent the various ruling factors in the town, and others in a purely social capacity as friends of the Mercers.

'Give him to me, dear, the moment you're tired,' muttered Lilian Mercer, and Avery smiled affectionately.

'Don't worry, Grandma, he's sleepy for the moment. You can have him if he yells.'

'When he does, let me have him, Lilian,' urged Hetty. 'You see more of him than I do.'

'No squabbling, ladies,' said Robert Mercer, chuckling. 'If he yells Charlie and I will take him for a walk.'

John Avery Charles Robert Mercer was behaving remarkably well, oblivious of the attention he was attracting on all sides as he lay cradled in the arms of his mother, who was wearing a slim crimson coat which kindled envy in the hearts of every female present.

Jonas Mercer bent to examine the small, sleeping face. 'Our son obviously possesses a sense of occasion,' he murmured. 'The speeches *are* likely to go on a bit. Are you bearing up, my darling?'

'Enjoying every minute,' Avery assured him with satisfaction. 'But before I unveil it I really should know what the plaque says.'

'It's a surprise. But you'll like it,' he assured her.

Eventually the last dignitary had had his say, Jonas made a brief, witty closing speech, and Avery relinquished her son to his grandmother. Her back very erect, she moved to the veiled plaque near the stairs to the auditorium and turned to face the onlookers.

'On behalf of the Mercom Group, it gives me great pleasure to declare the Stow Street Cinema open.' She tugged on the cord, the curtain drew back and Avery Mercer gazed in wonder at the inscription on the copper plate.

This building is dedicated to the memory of Ellen Crawford.

* * *

'I would have embraced the head honcho of Mercom with passionate appreciation then and there, but I felt we'd already caused enough excitement for one day,' said Avery when they got home that night.

'Pity,' said Jonas, watching his son make short work of his supper. 'I would have enjoyed that.'

'I can't describe how I felt when I saw those words, Jonas,' said Avery, as the last drop of milk left the bottle. She detached it from her son's sucking lips and held him up to pat him.

'I'll do that,' said Jonas, and held the baby against his bare shoulder. 'You look tired. We should have stayed with Frances and Philip and driven back tomorrow.'

'It's so complicated, staying with someone else with all the baby paraphernalia. Anyway, I wanted to get home—and Jay and I both slept like babies on the journey.'

Jonas looked at her over the small downy head of his son. 'You really think of this house as home, then?'

'Of course,' she said, surprised. 'Because it is our home—yours, mine and his nibs' here.'

Jonas kissed her, then chuckled at the sound of a great burp and handed his son to his mother. Avery praised her baby extravagantly, and carried him into the adjoining dressing room to put him down in his crib.

After a few minutes, to make sure he was settled, Avery returned to the bedroom and sat down at the dressing table to take down her hair and brush it loose—a nightly ritual her husband watched with his usual appreciation as they talked over the day. At last she turned out the light and slid in beside Jonas. 'Let's hope he sleeps for a while.'

'Are you tired, darling?'

'No. Much as I love him, I have other reasons for wanting our son to sleep.' She kissed the cheek she noticed her husband had taken the trouble to shave recently. 'You did a wonderful thing today, for me and my mother.'

'It was my personal tribute to two remarkable women,' said Jonas, returning the kiss.

'One I'll never forget.'

'I'm glad it made you happy.'

'I can't tell you how much.' Avery rubbed her cheek against his shoulder. 'Jonas.'

'Yes, my darling?'

'There's only one way I can think of to show my appreciation—'

'By making love to me?'

'That's my plan. Unless there's something else you'd prefer?'

He gave a deep, relishing sigh and held her close. 'Nothing in the world!'

UNCUT

Even more passion for your reading pleasure...

Escape into a world of intense passion and scorching
romance! You'll find the drama, the emotion, the
international settings and happy endings that you've
always loved in Harlequin Presents. But we've turned up
the thermostat just a little, so that the relationships really
sizzle.... Careful, they're almost too hot to handle!

This September, in

TAKEN FOR
HIS PLEASURE
by Carol Marinelli
(#2566)...

Sasha ran out on millionaire Gabriel Cabrini—
and he has never forgiven her. Now he wants
revenge.... But Sasha is determined not to
surrender again, no matter how persuasive
he may be....

**Also look for MASTER OF PLEASURE (#2571)
by bestselling author Penny Jordan.
Coming in October!**
www.eHarlequin.com

HPUC0906